'A delicate portrait of people inflicting subtle pain on others and themselves, and an appeal to the intelligent heart . . . full of metaphors that raise wry smiles . . . and lots of pert social commentary . . . This is literature to be read alone, curled up in the palm of an easy chair, with a Satie or Sade CD purring on the stereo . . . a moving still life' *Time*

'He very effectively observes the lonely shopgirl's dates, downfalls and searches for new antidepressants with sympathy and gentle humour. His vitriol is saved for his characteristic and entertaining assaults on the vacuities and superficialities of LA life' *The Times*

'A sensitive novella in which the occasional touches of humour are dry enough . . . to make it remarkably easy to forget that the author is a famous comedian . . . surprisingly well-observed story about loneliness, misunderstanding and love' *Daily Telegraph*

'*Shopgirl* is a witty, well-written and intelligent novella' *Times Literary Supplement*

'A melancholic, intricate love story about the hell men and women put each other through that's straight out of an old black and white movie . . . Carefully crafted and observed, Martin's making a point about the depths of his talent and feeling, and the shallowness of life in general' *Mirror*

'This beautifully written novel makes you think . . . by allowing you to watch the minutiae of someone else's life it makes you wish for something better' *B*

'A sensitive, original tale of loneliness and confusion in modern city life, lifted by tender humour'
Sunday Mirror

'Tender, observant and sharply witty, *Shopgirl* sprinkles fairy dust over an unlikely Los Angeles landscape'
Image

'Dry and dark on the outside, but with a sentimental soft heart, his novella is a creditable 'remake' of *Breakfast at Tiffany's*' *Esquire*

Steve Martin is one of today's most talented performers. He has had huge success as a film actor, with such credits as *Roxanne*, *Father of the Bride*, *Parenthood* and *The Spanish Prisoner*. He has won Emmys for his television writing and two Grammys for comedy albums. In addition to his bestselling collection of comic pieces, *Pure Drivel*, he has also written a play, *Picasso at the Lapin Agile*. His work appears in the *New Yorker* and *The New York Times*. He lives in Los Angeles.

BY STEVE MARTIN

Pure Drivel
Picasso at the Lapin Agile
Shopgirl

SHOPGIRL

STEVE MARTIN

PHŒNIX

A PHOENIX PAPERBACK

First published in Great Britain by Orion in 2001
This paperback edition published in 2001
by Phoenix,
an imprint of Orion Books Ltd,
Orion House, 5 Upper St Martin's Lane,
London WC2H 9EA

A CIP catalogue record for this book is available from the British Library.

ISBN 0 75381 283 5

Printed and bound in Great Britain by
Clays Ltd, St Ives plc

FOR ALLYSON

SHOPGIRL

When you work in the glove department at Neiman's, you are selling things that nobody buys anymore. These gloves aren't like the hard-working ones sold by L.L. Bean; these are so fine that a lady wearing them can still pick up a straight pin. The glove department is adjacent to the couture department and is really there for show. So a lot of Mirabelle's day is spent leaning against the glass case with one leg cocked behind her and her arms splayed outward, resting on her palms against the countertop. On an especially slow day she might lean over the case on her elbows – although this position is definitely not preferred by the management – and stare through the glass at the leather and silk gloves that lie on display like pristine, just-caught fish. The overhead lights reflect in the glass countertop and mingle with the gray and black of the gloves, resulting in a mother-of-pearl swirl that sometimes sends Mirabelle into a shallow hypnotic dream.

Everyone is silent at Neiman's, as though it were a religious site, and Mirabelle always tries to quiet the tap-tap-tapping of her heels when she walks across the percussive marble floors. If you saw her, you would assume by her gait that she is in danger of slipping at any moment. However, this is the way Mirabelle walks all the time, even on the sure friction of a concrete sidewalk. She has simply never quite learned to walk or hold herself comfortably, which makes her come off as an attractive wallflower. For Mirabelle, the high point of working at a department store is that she gets to dress up to go to work, as the Neiman's dress code encourages her to be a model of precision and style. Her problem, of course, is paying for the clothes that she favors, but one way or another, helped out by a generous employee discount and a knack for mixing and matching a recycled dress with a 50 percent off Armani sweater, she manages to dress well without straining her budget.

Every day at lunchtime she walks around the corner into Beverly Hills to the Time Clock Café, which offers her a regular lunch at a nominal price. One sandwich, which always amounts to three dollars and seventy-five cents, a side salad, and a drink, and she can keep her tab just under her preferred six-dollar maximum, which can surge to nearly eight dollars if she opts for dessert. Sometimes, a man whose name she overheard once – Tom, she thinks it is – will eye her legs, which show off nicely as she sits at a wrought-iron table so shallow it forces her to angle them out into the aisle. Mirabelle, who never takes credit for her attractiveness, believes it is not she he is responding to but rather something independent of her, like the lovely line her fine blue skirt makes as it cuts diagonally across the white of her thigh.

The rest of the day at Neiman's sees her leaning or bending or rearranging, with the occasional odd customer pulling her out of the afternoon's slow motion until 6 p.m. finally ticks over. She then closes the register and walks over to the elevator, her upper body rigid. She descends to the first floor and passes the glistening perfume counters, where the salesgirls stay a full half hour after closing to accommodate late buyers, and where by now, the various scents that have been sprayed throughout the day onto waiting customers have collected into strata in the department store air. So Mirabelle, at five-six, always smells Chanel number 5, while someone at five-two is always treated to the heavier Chanel number 19. This daily walk always reminds her that she works in the Siberia of Neiman's, the isolated, landlocked glove department, and she wonders when she will be moved around in the hierarchy to at least perfume, because there, in the energetic, populated worlds of cosmetics and aromatics, she can get that which she wants more than anything: someone to talk to.

Depending on the time of year, Mirabelle's drive home offers either the sunny evening light of summer or the early darkness and halogen headlights of winter in Pacific standard time. She traverses Beverly Boulevard, the chameleon street with elegant furniture stores and restaurants on one end and Vietnamese shops selling mysterious packaged roots on the other. In fifteen miles, like a Monopoly game in reverse, this street dwindles in property value and ends at her second-story apartment in Silverlake, an artists' community that is always bordering on being dangerous but never quite succeeding. Some evenings, if the timing is right, she can climb the outdoor stairs to her walk-up and catch L.A.'s most beautiful sight: a Pacific sunset cumulating over the spread of lights that flows from her front-door stoop to the sea. She then enters her apartment, which for no good reason doesn't have a window to the view, and the disappearing sun finally blackens everything outside, transforming her windows into mirrors.

Mirabelle has two cats. One is normal, the other is a reclusive kitten who lives under a sofa and rarely comes out. *Very* rarely. Once a year. This gives Mirabelle the feeling that there is a mysterious stranger living in her apartment whom she never sees but who leaves evidence of his existence by subtly moving small, round objects from room to room. This description could easily apply to Mirabelle's few friends, who also leave evidence of their existence, in missed phone messages and rare get-togethers, and are also seldom seen. This is because they view her as an oddnik, and their failure to include her leaves her alone on many nights. She knows that she needs new friends but introductions are hard to come by when your natural state is shyness.

Mirabelle replaces the absent friends with books and television mysteries of the PBS kind. The books are mostly nineteenth-century novels in which women are poisoned or are doing the poisoning. She does not read these books as a romantic lonely hearts turning pages in the isolation of her room, not at all. She is instead an educated spirit with a sense of irony. She loves the gloom of these period novels, especially as kitsch, but beneath it all she finds that a part of her identifies with all that darkness.

There is something else, too: Mirabelle can draw. Her output is small in quantity and size. Only a few four-by-five-inch drawings are finished in a year, and they are infused with the eerie spirit of the mysteries she reads. She densely coats the paper with a black waxy crayon, covering everything except the image she wants to reveal, which appears to be floating up through the blackness. Her latest is a rendering of a crouching child charred stiff in the lava of Pompeii. Her drawing hand is sure, trained in the years she spent acquiring a master of fine arts degree at a California college while incurring thirty-nine thousand dollars of debt from student loans. This degree makes her a walking anomaly among the perfume girls and shoe clerks at Neiman's, whose highest accomplishments are that they were cute in high school. Rarely, but often enough to have a small collection of her own work, Mirabelle gets out the charcoals and pulls the kitchen lamp down low, near the hard surface of her breakfast table, and makes a drawing. It is then properly fixed and photographed and stowed away in a professional portfolio. These nights of drawing leave her exhausted, for they require the full concentration of her energy, and on those evenings she stumbles to bed and falls into a dead sleep.

On a normal night, her routine is very simple, involving the application of lotion to her body while chattering to the visible kitten, with occasional high-voiced interjections to the assumed cat under the sofa. If there were a silent observer, Mirabelle would be seen as a carefree, happy girl who is preparing for a night on the town. But in reality, these activities are the physical manifestations of her stillness.

Tonight, as the evening closes, Mirabelle slips into bed, says an audible good night to both cats, and shuts her eyes. Her hand clicks off the lamp next to her, and her head fills with ghosts. Now her mind can wander in any landscape it desires, and she makes a nightly ritual of these waking dreams. She sees herself standing on the edge of a tropical lagoon. A man comes up from behind her, wraps his arms around her, buries his face in her neck, and whispers, "don't move." The image generates a damp first molecule of wetness between her legs, and she presses her bladed hand between them, and falls asleep.

In the morning, the dry food that had been laid out in a bowl the night before is now gone, more evidence of the phantom cat. Mirabelle, sleepy eyed and still groggy, prepares her breakfast and takes her Serzone.

The Serzone is a gift from God that frees her from the immobilizing depression that would otherwise surround her and seep into her body like a poisonous fog. The drug distances the depression from her, although it is never out of sight. It is also the third mood elevator that she has tried in as many years. The first two worked, and worked well for a while, then abruptly dropped her. There is always a struggle as the new drug, which for a while has to be blended with the old one, takes root in her brain and begins to work its mysterious chemistry.

The depression she battles is not the newly acquired symptom of a young woman now living in Los Angeles on her own. It was first set in the bow in Vermont, where she grew up, and fired as a companion arrow that has traveled with her ever since. With the drug, she is generally able to corner it and keep it separate from her daily life. There are black stretches, however, when she is unable to move from her bed. She takes full advantage of the sick days that are built into her work allowances at Neiman's.

In spite of her depression, Mirabelle likes to think of herself as humorous. She can, when the occasion calls, become a wisecracker and buoyant party girl. This mood, Mirabelle thinks, sometimes makes her the center of attention at parties and gatherings. The truth is that these episodes of gaiety merely raise her to normal, but for Mirabelle the feeling is so exceptional that she believes herself to be standing out. The power at these parties remains with the neurotically spirited women, who attract men whose need it is to tame them. Mirabelle attracts men of a different kind. They are shyer and more reticent. They look at her a long time before approaching, and when they do find something about her that they want, it is something simple within her.

JEREMY

At twenty-six, Jeremy is two years younger than Mirabelle. He grew up in the slacker-based L.A. high school milieu, where aspiration languishes and the lucky ones get kick-started in their first year of college by an enthused and charismatic professor. He had no college dreams and hence no proximity to the challenge of new faces and ideas – he currently stencils logos on amplifiers for a living – and Jeremy's life after high school slid sideways on an imperceptibly canted icy slope, angling away from center. It is appropriate that he and Mirabelle met at a Laundromat, the least noir dating arena on earth. Their first encounter began with "hey," and ended with a loose "see ya," as Mirabelle stood amidst her damp underwear and jogging shorts.

Jeremy took Mirabelle on approximately two and a half dates. The half date was actually a full evening, but was so vaporous that Mirabelle had trouble counting it as a full unit. On the first, which consisted mainly of shuffling around a shopping mall while Jeremy tried to graze her ass with the back of his hand, he split the dinner bill with her and then, when she suggested they actually go inside the movie theatre whose new neon front so transfixed Jeremy, made her pay for her own ticket. Mirabelle could not afford to go out again under the same circumstances, and there was no simple way to explain this to him. The conversation at dinner hadn't been successful either; it bore the marks of an old married couple who had very little left to say to each other. After walking her to her door, he gave her his phone number, in a peculiar reversal of dating procedure. She might have considered kissing him, even after the horrible first date, but he just didn't seem to know what to do. However, Jeremy does have one outstanding quality. He likes her. And this quality in a person makes them infinitely interesting to the person who is being liked. At the end of their first date, as she stepped inside her apartment and her hand was delivering the door to its jamb, there was a slight pause, and they exchanged a quick look of inexplicable intent. Once inside, instead of forever losing his number in her coat pocket, she absentmindedly stuck it under her phone.

Six days after their first date, which had cut Mirabelle's net worth by 20 percent, she runs into Jeremy again at the Laundromat. He waves at her, gives her the thumbs-up sign, then watches her as she loads clothes into the machines. He seems unable to move, but speaks just loudly enough for his voice to carry over twelve clanking washing machines, "Did you watch the game last night?" Mirabelle is shocked when she later learns that Jeremy considers this their second date. This fact comes out when at one abortive get-together, Jeremy invokes the "third date" rule, believing he should be received at second base. Mirabelle is not fooled by any such third date rule, and she explains to Jeremy that she cannot conceive of any way their Laundromat encounter, or any encounter involving the thumbs-up sign, can be considered a date.

This third date is also problematic because after warning Jeremy that she is not going to pay half of its cost, she is taken to a bowling alley and forced to pay for her own rental shoes. Jeremy explains that bowling shoes are an article of clothing, and he certainly can't be expected to pay for what she wears on a date. If only Jeremy's logical mind could be applied to astrophysics and not rental shoes, he would now be a honcho at NASA. He does cough up for dinner and several games, even though he uses discount coupons clipped from the newspaper to help pay for it all. Finally, Mirabelle suggests that if they have future dates, he should take her phone number, call her, and they could do free things. Mirabelle knows, and she lets this be unspoken, that all free things require conversation. Sitting in a darkened movie theatre requires absolutely no conversation at all, whereas a free date, like a walk down Hollywood Boulevard in the busy evening, requires comments, chatter, observations, and with luck, wit. She worries that since they have only exchanged perhaps two dozen words between them, these free dates will be horrible.

She is still willing to go out with him, however, until something less horrible comes along.

Jeremy's attraction to Mirabelle arises from her passing similarity to someone he had fallen in love with in his preadolescent life. This person is Popeye's girlfriend, Olive Oyl, whom he used to swoon over in a few antique comic books lent to him by his uncle. And yes, Mirabelle does bear some similarity, but only after the suggestion is made. You would not walk into a room, see her for the first time, and think *Olive Oyl.* However, once the idea is proposed, one's response might be a long, slow, "ahhhh ... yes." She has a long thin body, two small dark eyes, and a small red mouth. She also dresses like Olive Oyl, in fitted clothes – never a fluffy, girly dress – and she holds herself like Ms. Oyl, too, in a kind of jangle. Olive Oyl has no breasts, but Mirabelle does, though the way she carries herself, with her shoulders folded, in clothing that never accentuates her curves, makes her appear flat. All this in no way discounts her attractiveness. Mirabelle is attractive; it's just that she is never the first or second girl chosen. But to Jeremy, Mirabelle's most striking resemblance to Olive Oyl is her translucent skin. It recalls for him the pale skin of the cartoon figure, which was actually the creamy paper showing from underneath.

Jeremy's thought process is so thin that he has the happy consequence of always ending up doing exactly what he wants to do at all times. He never complicates a desire by overthinking it, unlike Mirabelle, who spins a cocoon around an idea until it is immobile. His view of the world is one that keeps his blood pressure low, sweeping the cholesterol from his relaxed, freeway-sized arteries. Everyone knows he is going to live till age ninety, although the question that goes begging is, "for what?"

Jeremy and Mirabelle are separated by a hundred million miles of vacuum space. He falls asleep at night in blissful ignorance. She, subtly doped on her prescription, time-travels through the terrain of her unconscious until she is overcome by sleep. He knows only what is right in front of him; she is aware of every incoming sensation that glances obliquely against her soft, fragile core. At this stage of their lives, in true and total fact, the only thing they have in common is a Laundromat.

MIRABELLE'S FRIDAY

She stands over the glove counter, and from her secluded outpost looks far across the hall toward the couture department. When the view is reversed, and a couture girl bothers to glance toward her, Mirabelle looks like a puppy standing on its hind legs, and the two brown dots of her eyes, set in the china plate of her face, make her seem very cute and noticeable. But pointlessly so, at least today. For this Friday is what she has termed the day of the dead, when for some reason – usually an upcoming Beverly Hills dress-up event – the couture department fills with women who are unlikely to notice the slender girl standing at one end of their hallowed hall. They are the Wives of Important Men.

The metamorphosis most wanted by the wives of important men is that they become important in their own right. This distinction is achieved by wielding power over any and all and is characterized by an intense obsession with spending. Without spending, there would be thirty to sixty empty hours per week, to be filled with what? And not only is there the spending itself, there is the organization and management of spending. There is hiring and firing, there is the discernment of what the spending needs to be on, and there is the psychological requirement that the husband be proud of the wife's spending. The range of the spending can go from clothes and jewelry to furniture and lighting, dishes and flatware, and catalogue seeds and firewood. Sometimes it is fun to spend economically. Of course, economic spending is not intended to save money, but is a practice of ethics.

Along with the desire to spend comes a desire to control what is coming back at them from the mirror. Noses are bobbed into a shape that nature never knew, hair is whipped up with air and colored into a metallic tinted meringue, and faces are pulled into death masks. The variety of alteration is vast, except when it comes to breasts. Breasts are made large only – and in the process misshapen – and the incongruity of two bowling balls on an ironing board never seems to bother anyone. In Beverly Hills, young men, searching for young women who remind them of their face-lifted mothers, are stranded and forlorn in a sea of natural-looking twenty-five-year-olds.

Today, as she stares hypnotically at these tribal women, one clear thought emerges to Mirabelle: how different this place is from Vermont. Then, out of the idleness that permeates every day at work, she shifts her weight from one foot to the other. She scratches her elbow. She curls her toes, then angles her leg to give her calf a stretch. She flicks a paper clip several inches across the glass of the countertop. She runs her tongue along the back of her teeth. Footsteps approach her. Her automatic response is to straighten up and look like she is an ever ready force in the Neiman's sales team, for the sound of footsteps could mean *supervisor* as likely as *customer*. What she sees, though, is a rare sight in the fourth-floor glove department. It is a gentleman, looking for a pair of ladies' dress gloves. He wants them gift wrapped and could they do that? Mirabelle nods in her professional way, and then the man, sharply dressed in a dark blue suit, asks her opinion on which is the finest pair. Being a sharp dresser herself, she actually does have an opinion on the merchandise she offers, and she gives him the lowdown on smart glove purchasing. There is some conversation about what and who they are for. The man gives her some embarrassed, vague answers, often the case when men shop for women, and in response she suggests that the silver satin Diors are the best. He purchases the gloves with a credit card, smiles at her, and leaves. Mirabelle watches him walk away. Her eyes go to his shoes, which she understands and knows something about, and her inner checklist gives him full marks in all categories. Mirabelle catches herself in the countertop mirror, and realizes she has blushed.

There are a few late browsers that day, and they punctuate the tedium like drops from a Chinese water torture. Six o'clock, and she is down the stairs rather than the elevator, which can become clogged at closing time, and out onto the main floor. Several customers linger at the fragrance counter, a few in cosmetics, surprisingly light for a Friday. Mirabelle thinks the salesgirls in these departments overuse their own products, especially the lipstick. With their inclination toward the heavy application of a greasy burgundy, they look like Man Ray's disembodied lips floating over a landscape of boxed perfumes.

It is six-fifteen and pitch dark on the drive home down Beverly Boulevard. It is drizzling rain, which causes the traffic to move like sludge in a trough. Mirabelle wears her driving glasses as she grips the wheel with both hands. She drives in the same posture as she walks, overly erect. The glasses give her a librarian quality – before libraries were on CD-ROM – and the '89 Toyota truck she drives indicates a librarian's salary, too. The rain splashes on the roof and Garrison Keillor intones on the radio, creating a warm, fireside feeling in this unlikeliest of circumstances. All this coziness sends her into a little ache and she swears that she will find someone tonight to hold her. This is an extremely rare decision for Mirabelle. The last time she was even mildly promiscuous was in college, when it was the thing to do and she was feeling her bohemian oats. She decides that when she gets home, she will pick up the phone and call Jeremy.

SLEEPING WITH JEREMY

In calling Jeremy, Mirabelle knows that she is making a devil's bargain. She is offering herself to him on the outside chance that he will hold her afterward. She feels very practical about this and vows not to feel bad if things don't work out. After all, she tells herself, she isn't really involved with him emotionally or otherwise.

For Mirabelle, there are four levels of being held. The first, and highest, is the complete surround: he will wrap his arms around her and they will spoon as he whispers how beautiful she is and how he had been transported to another plane. The odds of this particular scenario unfolding from the youthful Jeremy are slim, in fact, so slim that they could slip out the door without opening it. There are, however, other levels of holding that for tonight would suit Mirabelle just fine. He could lie on his back and she would rest her head on his chest, while one of his arms holds her tight. Third best would involve Mirabelle lying on her back with Jeremy alongside her, resting one hand on her stomach while the other plays with her hair. This position requires the utterances of sweet nothings for her to be fully satisfied. She is aware he has barely spoken a sentence that didn't end in "you know" and then trail off into a mumble since they have been together, which makes the appearance of these sweet nothings unlikely. But this could be a plus, as she can interpret his mumbles any way she wants – they could be impeccably metered love sonnets for all she knows. In fourth position, they are lying on their backs, with one of Jeremy's legs resting languidly over one of hers. This is the minimally acceptable outcome, and involves a commitment of extra time on his part to compensate for his lack of effort.

Coming out of her reverie, which was so specific she could have been a lawyer formulating a contract, she picks up the phone and dials. It rings a few times, and the thought that he might not be home sends a shiver of relief through her. However, just as she is about to hang up, she hears the clatter of the phone being picked up. But instead of hearing his voice on the other end of the line, she hears what she makes out to be Jeremy's TV set filtered through the telephone. She keeps waiting for him to say hello or yeah or anything, but the TV continues. Eventually she hears him walk across the room, open the refrigerator, walk back to the living room, and flop himself down on the sofa. She can hear the laugh track of the television, and a few moments later, Jeremy's vociferous nose-blow. Mirabelle stands there, wondering what to do. She thinks surely he will see that the phone is off the hook. Surely he heard it ring. Now committed, she worries that if she hangs up, she will get a busy signal for the rest of the night, as it is already clear that the phone doesn't lie in the path from sofa to refrigerator, and that that particular route is the only one he will be taking that evening. She presses the speakerphone button and cradles the handset. Jeremy's TV is still present in her house, but at least she has her hands free.

In her small apartment she is never far from the speaker, and she gets out of her shoes and takes off her skirt and blouse, throws on an oversized shirt, and walks around in her underwear. She completes several chores that are left over from the weekend. A couple of times she screams Jeremy's name into the speakerphone, with no effect. She catches herself midscream and thinks how it must look and swears never to do something so humiliating again for any reason, ever, in her life. Then, with the TV still squawking through the telephone, she sits back on her futon and starts to laugh. The laughter causes a few tears to appear at the corners of her eyes, which sets her off on a crying jag. Then a hiccup gets her laughing again, causing her to fall over sideways on the futon, and at one point she is actually laughing and crying at the same time. She finally burns herself out and after resting for several minutes, goes over to hang up the phone. As she is about to press the hope-ending speaker button, she hears Jeremy's footsteps coming across the hardwood, increasing in volume, clearly walking toward the phone. Her hand hesitates. Then she hears the touch-tones of Jeremy dialing the phone. She waits. Suddenly his voice says, "Hello?" Mirabelle picks up the receiver and says hello back.

"It's Jeremy."

She responds, "Do you know who this is?"

"Yeah. Mirabelle."

"Did you just call me?" she says.

"Yeah."

It is at this point that she understands that Jeremy knows nothing about what has occurred over the last twenty minutes. He thinks he has just walked over to the phone and dialed Mirabelle, and she has answered. Mirabelle decides not to ask what happened, afraid that they might enter an infinite loop of explanation. It turns out that he wants to see her that night, so she invites him over and everything falls into place.

Jeremy arrives thirty minutes later and leans against the wall with a slouch so extreme that he appears to have left his skeleton at home. He carries a paper bag containing some vile-smelling fast food, which she immediately recognizes as French fries because the grease stains have made the bag transparent. But at least he's had the courtesy to bring something over, an offering to her for what he is about to receive. Mirabelle hastily constructs a fifth option, which is to get him to simply snuggle with her, so she won't have to put out. This option is hastily discarded because it is the afterglow she wants, and she begins her process of seduction wordlessly, naturally set into motion by the blush of her skin, and the willingness of her legs, and her readiness, which she knows a man can sense. If only Jeremy were a man.

Instead, she practically has to spell it out for him. Mirabelle longs to have a *Wuthering Heights* movie on tape that she can throw on, point to, and say, "Get it?" Jeremy's instinct for lovemaking turns out to be all right, once the idea has been writ large by Mirabelle with oils and candles and incense and music and some two-bit scotch that neither has drunk before in their lives. But because Jeremy fails to fully arouse Mirabelle, her ardor never peaks and she therefore fails to fully arouse Jeremy, resulting in a see-saw condom battle that is waged this way: she works Jeremy up into a nice little erection, but by the time they get the condom on, with its dulling insulation, there is a loss of stature. Mirabelle is not exactly relaxed and wet either, which causes Jeremy's penis to bend and fold as he tries to enter her. Then they have to start all over. She removes the condom, works him up by kissing him on the mouth and stimulating him with her hand. Occasionally, the cat jumps on the bed and bats at Jeremy's testicles as if they were hanging balls of catnip, causing a disastrous delay in the action. Then they struggle with the condom and the cycle begins all over again. This goes back and forth several times, with Mirabelle rubbing him vigorously, then flopping herself speedily back on the bed and spreading her legs instantly, until the inevitable happens again. There are three entities in the room that night, Mirabelle,

Jeremy, and an animated penis that expands and contracts like an anesthesiologist's oxygen balloon. Finally, his youth prevails, and Jeremy successfully dwells for a few moments in paradise. The life expectancy of a radial tire: this is the thought that races through Jeremy's mind as he tries to delay his impatient ejaculation.

Eventually, the deed is done and all the thrashing comes to an end. The two of them, not touching, lie there in the shadowy darkness, and everything is silent. The distance between them is awful. But then Jeremy snakes his arm around her shoulder, sliding it just under her neck, and reaches his hand up into her hair and gently pulls her near him. He brings his body in close. Mirabelle feels her perspiration mix with his, and she likes that. Her senses refocus on the room and she smells the vanilla of the candle. She sees herself in the bedroom mirror and notices that her breasts have filled from his touch, clumsy as it was, and she likes the way she looks. Jeremy glistens in the low light. Mirabelle stares into her own eyes. And she feels all right.

Then a terrible thing happens. Jeremy uncoils himself from Mirabelle, stands in his underwear at the foot of the bed, and begins to talk. More than talk. Orate. And worse, he talks in a way that requires Mirabelle to respond with periodic uh-huhs. What he talks about is a range of topics loosely categorized under the heading Jeremy. He talks about Jeremy's hopes and dreams, his likes and dislikes, and, unfortunately, a lot about amplifiers. This includes Jeremy's perspective on amplifiers, and cost analysis, and how his boss's view of amplifiers contrasts with his own. This is the topic that requires most of the uh-huhs, and only by staring straight at him and forcing her eyes open a tiny bit wider, can Mirabelle appear somewhat interested. Unlike his penis, his stream of chatter does not rise and fall. It maintains a steady flow, and Mirabelle begins to question whether William Jennings Bryan still deserves to be known as America's most grandiose public speaker. Jeremy booms and bellows opinions and observations for a full thirty minutes, none of which ever leave the sphere of Jeremy. Eventually, he sputters out, returns to bed, and puts an arm around her, in a position yet uncategorized by Mirabelle that gives her some more of what she wants. Even with the ignoble flailing that took place earlier, she feels as though she has been wanted, and she knows he has thought her beautiful, and that she has made him happy and energized him, and that the expenditure of his energy on her has sent him into a deep, deep sleep.

THE WEEKEND

It is 9 a.m., and for the second time that morning Mirabelle is awake. The first time was two hours earlier when Jeremy slipped out, giving her a kiss good-bye that was so formal it might as well have been wearing a tuxedo. She didn't take it badly because, well, she couldn't afford to. She also is glad he's gone, not looking forward to the awkward task of getting to know a man she's already slept with. A little eye of sunlight forms on her bed and inches its way across her bedspread. She gets up, mixes her Serzone into a glass of orange juice, and drinks it down as though it were a quick vodka tonic, fortifying herself for the weekend.

Weekends can be dangerous for someone of Mirabelle's fragility. One little slipup in scheduling and she can end up staring at eighteen hours of television. That's why she joined a volunteer organization that goes out and builds and repairs houses for the disadvantaged, a kind of community cleanup operation, called Habitat for Humanity. This takes care of the day. Saturday night usually offers a spontaneous get-together with the other

Habitat workers in a nearby bar. If that doesn't happen, which this night it doesn't, Mirabelle is not afraid to go to a local bar alone, which this night she does, where she might run into someone she knows or nurse a drink and listen to the local band. As she sits in a booth and checks the amplifiers for Jeremy's signature stencil, it never occurs to her to observe herself, and thus she is spared the image of a girl sitting alone in a bar on Saturday night. A girl who is willing to give every ounce of herself to someone, who could never betray her lover, who never suspects maliciousness of anyone, and whose sexuality sleeps in her, waiting to be stirred. She never feels sorry for herself, except when the overpowering chemistry of depression inundates her and leaves her helpless. She moved from Vermont hoping to begin her life, and now she is stranded in the vast openness of L.A. She keeps working to make connections, but the pile of near misses is starting to overwhelm her. What Mirabelle needs is some omniscient voice to illuminate and spotlight her, and to inform everyone that this one has value, this one over here, the one sitting in the bar by herself, and then to find her counterpart and bring him to her.

But that night, the voice does not come, and she quietly folds herself up and leaves the bar.

The voice is to come on Tuesday.

MONDAY

Mirabelle awakes to a crisp L.A. day with an ice blue chill in the air. The view from her apartment is of both mountains and sea, but she can see it only by peering around her front door. She feeds the cats, drinks her potion, and puts on her best underwear – although it is unlikely anyone will see it today, unless someone bursts in on her in a changing room. She had a nice day on Sunday because her friends Loki and Del Rey finally called back and invited her to brunch at one of the outdoor cafés on Western. They gossiped and talked, about the men in their lives, about who is gay and who isn't, about who is a coke head and who is promiscuous, and Mirabelle regaled them with the Jeremy story. Loki and Del Rey, who were obviously named by parents who thought they would never not be infants, told similar stories and the three of them cried with laughter. This buoyed Mirabelle, as it made her feel normal, like one of the girls. But when she went home that night, she wondered if she had betrayed Jeremy just a little, as something in her believed that he would not have told about their exploits over lunch with the guys. This little thought was a tiny foundation for Jeremy's tiny redemption, and it made part of her like him, if only just a little bit.

๑

The day at Neiman's plods along, made extra viscous by the promise of a fun evening with the girls. It is Art Walk night in Los Angeles, when the town's galleries stay open and offer free "wine" in plastic cups. Most of the local artists will be spotted tonight at one gallery or another. Mirabelle's own talent for drawing makes her feel comfortable and confident in this group, and having recently placed several of her recent works with a local gallery makes her feel that she is an equal.

Finally, six o'clock. Tonight's walk past cosmetics and perfumes has special fascination for Mirabelle. Being Monday, there are no customers and the she-clerks are idle. Mirabelle notices that when they are in motion, these perfume nymphs look breezy and alive, but when they are still, their faces become vacuous and frozen, like the Easter Island of the Barbie Dolls. She then retrieves her truck from the dungeon of the parking garage, slams it into fourth, does her thing down Beverly Boulevard, and is home in nineteen minutes.

At eight minutes after seven, she hits the Bentley Gallery on Robertson where she is to meet Loki and

Del Rey. The joint is not jumping but at least it has enough people in it so everyone is forced to raise his voice, giving the impression of an event. Mirabelle wears her tight maroon knee-length skirt over low heels and a smart white sweater that sets off her blunt-cut nut-brown hair. Loki and Del Rey aren't there yet, and Mirabelle has the annoying thought that they might not show. It wouldn't be the first time they'd left her stranded. As Mirabelle never shows her distress, it is assumed she is fine in all circumstances and Loki and Del Rey never figure that their failure to show is really a thoughtless ditching. She gets a plastic cup of wine and does the thing she always does at these openings, something so odd that it sets her apart from all the others. She looks at the paintings. It is a perfect disguise. Holding the wine dictates her posture so she doesn't have to think about where to put her hands, and the pictures on the walls give her something to focus on while she stands sentry for Loki and Del Rey.

Twenty minutes later, the two women appear, snag Mirabelle, and head two blocks up to Fire, an avant-garde gallery – or at least one that thinks it is. This opening has more of the party atmosphere that everyone is looking for, and some of the revelers have even spilled out onto the street. For Loki and Del Rey, this is the warm-up party for their final landing spot, the Reynaldo Gallery. The Reynaldo Gallery, representing the big money artists, is set in the heart of Beverly Hills and needs the prettiest girls and the most relevant people to populate its openings. After getting enough alcohol at the Fire Gallery to hold them – they know the bar at Reynaldo's will be impossible – they drive into Beverly Hills, park and lock, and cross Santa Monica Boulevard to the gallery. They push their way in and finally slink through the crowd and into the heart of the matter. The party needs a volume control but there isn't one, and everyone would be straining to hear each other except they are all talking simultaneously. Loki and Del Rey decide to brave the tumult at the bar, and at first Mirabelle hangs loosely by them, but eventually the chaos separates them and she finds herself in the vacant narrow rim that circles the room between the crowd and the paintings. Only this time she is less intent on the pictures and more intent on who and what is going on in the room. In a sea of black dresses, she is the only one wearing any color, and she is the only one wearing almost no makeup, including the men. Her eyes scan the room and spot several celebrities dressed in the latest nomad/wanderer fashion and several very handsome men who have learned to give off the seductive impression that they would be consummate fathers.

One in particular attracts her, one who looks as though he does not know he is handsome, who looks slightly lost and like an actual working artist, whom she dubs the Artist/Hero. She sees him notice her staring, so she skillfully moves her eyes away, where she sees the absolute opposite of his pleasure-giving radiance. It is Lisa. Lisa is one of the cosmetics girls at Neiman's, and

Mirabelle can't help but recoil. What is she doing here? This girl does not belong at an art opening. She is on Mirabelle's turf, where an eked-out high school diploma is just not enough. But Lisa holds her own, and here's why. Lisa, thirty-two, can be counted among the very beautiful. She has pale red hair that hangs in soft ringlets against skin that has never seen the sun. She is slender and oval faced, with shapely legs that pin themselves into a pair of provocative high heels. Her breasts, though augmented, rise above the line of her dress and seem to beckon, successfully keeping the secret of their artificiality. She appears sunny, a quality that Mirabelle can call upon only for special occasions.

Lisa wears high heels even to lunch. In fact, she overdresses for every occasion, because without the splash that her wardrobe makes, she believes that no man will like her. She fools herself by thinking that in some way she is pursuing a career by making important contacts with successful men, and that the sex is tangential. The men play along, too. They think that she likes them, that her hand jobs aren't bought. These men allow her to feel interesting. After all, aren't they listening to every word? She believes that only in her body's perfection can she be loved, and her diet focuses on five imaginary pounds that keep her from perfection. This weight anxiety is not negotiable. No convincing makes it otherwise, even from the most sincere of her lovers. Lisa's idea of fun is going to bars and taunting college men by making them believe she is available. A good time is measured by the abandon she can muster; the more people who are crammed into a Mercedes heading to a party in the hills, the more valid the proof that she is having fun. At thirty-two, Lisa does not know about forty, and she is unprepared for the time when she will actually have to know something in order to have people listen to her. Her penalty is that the men she attracts with her current package see her only from a primitive part of their brains, the childish part that likes shiny objects that make noise when rattled. Older men looking for playthings and callow boys driven by hormones access these areas more easily than the clear-thinking wife seekers of their late twenties and early thirties.

There is a third category of men who like Lisa. These are the men whose relationship to women is driven by obsession and possession, and she will be the ugly target of more than one such man in her lifetime. To Mirabelle, the idea of being an object of obsession is alluring and represents a powerful love. She fails to understand, however, that men become obsessive over beautiful women because they want no one else to have them, but they fall in love with women like Mirabelle because they want a certain, specific part of them.

Mirabelle turns away, refusing to be intimidated by this crimson Marilyn. She is staring at the surface of a picture when she overhears voices in conversation next to her. Two men are trying to remember the name of the artist who uses words in his paintings. She quickly discounts the New York artist Roy Lichtenstein as the conversation is on the wrong coast.

"Are you thinking of Ed Ruscha?" says Mirabelle.

Both men snap their fingers and begin a conversation with her. After two sentences, she realizes that one of them is the impossibly perfect, lost-looking Artist / Hero that she had spotted only minutes earlier. This provokes a certain eloquence in Mirabelle, at least in terms of L.A. art, which she keeps up on through gallery visits and reviews, and she presents herself to the Artist/Hero as formidable and worthwhile and smart. So Mirabelle doesn't flinch when Lisa walks over, and she accepts her into the group, giving Lisa a generous benefit of the doubt. She isn't really aware that Lisa has already taken over the conversation with her flashing eyes and pointed laughter, and has slipped in between the cracks of the Artist/Hero's brain with the subliminal suggestion that she likes him, and likes him a lot. By appealing to his absolute worst side, Lisa eventually dominates him, and later the Artist/Hero is seen taking her phone number. Mirabelle is not affected by a man's failure to approach her, as her own self-deprecating attitude never allows the idea that he would in the first place.

Mirabelle does not understand that Lisa's maneuvering is not directed at the Artist/Hero, but at her. She does not see that she has been defeated by an opponent who wants to see the glove girl in retreat. In Lisa's mind, she has once again established the superiority of the cosmetics department over the glove department, and by association, the couture department itself.

Mirabelle participates in several other good conversations throughout the rest of the evening. The thoughtful nature of these exchanges makes her feel that this is exactly what she should be doing and that she couldn't be doing anything better. After being dropped off by Loki and Del Rey at gallery number one to get her car, she drives home, her head filled with recapitulations of the evening's finest arguments in order to find out whom she agrees with most.

She slides into bed at exactly midnight, after amusing herself by feeding her cats with a bowl that says "good dog." She closes her eyes and taps her finger on the lamp switch. A few moments later, as she lies quiescent in her bed, she feels something terrible enter her brain, stay for a fleeting second, then disappear. She does not know what it is, only that she doesn't like it.

TUESDAY

It is now the middle of November, and the smell of Thanksgiving is in the air, which means that Christmas is waiting in the oven. The increasing number of browsers forces Mirabelle to forgo her favorite position of leaning over the counter on her elbows, something she can get away with only when there are absolutely no customers in sight.

She skips lunch because she has to visit Dr. Tracy to renew her Serzone. He asks her several questions that she correctly answers, and he writes out the prescription. She feels relieved, as her supply seems dangerously low, and is glad to have the prescription overlap by several weeks instead of four days. She worries about unforeseen events like the doctor suddenly having to be out of town, leaving her short. She also renews her prescription for birth control pills, which she takes not especially for birth control but more for her period, which in the past has been uncomfortably nonperiodic.

The rest of the day at Neiman's seems like purgatory as tonight there is no Art Walk to look forward to; there is nothing. Her plan is to read, perhaps draw, or find an old movie on the classics channel. Maybe she can put together a phone call between herself and Loki. By the end of the day, her lower back aches and her soles burn. She prepares the register a full half hour before closing, knowing there are to be no more customers. All she has to do when six o'clock strikes is press one button and the register is closed. She is satisfyingly out minutes early, and in her car.

The streets of Los Angeles are starting to crowd regularly now in anticipation of the holidays. Even the shortcuts are clogging up, and Mirabelle uses the time in her car to plan the coming months. From Christmas Day to New Year's Day she will be in Vermont visiting her parents and brother. She already has the airplane ticket, bought months earlier at a phenomenally low price. Thanksgiving is still open, and she knows it needs to be filled. To be alone on Thanksgiving is a kind of death sentence. The year before it had been commuted at the last minute by a visiting uncle who happened to be in town and who invited her to a small gathering at a restaurant, and then hit on her. This had been a particularly grim evening as the dinner company had also been lousy. They were a stuffy group who were having steaks and cigarettes, who were united by a rare quality on this day: they were thankless. The seldom-seen uncle on the mother's side then drove her home, high as a kite, and under the pretense of fingering her pretty necklace, laid the back of his hand on her blouse, then asked if he could come in. Mirabelle looked at him dead in the eye and said, "I'll tell Mom." The uncle feigned ignorance, drunkenly walked her to the door, returned to his car, put it in reverse when he intended drive, and fled.

Mirabelle suddenly finds herself home, having no recollection of any detail of the drive from Neiman's. She parks her car in the spot reserved for her in the clapboard garage. She lugs a bag of groceries, her purse, and an empty cardboard box up the two short flights to her insular apartment, which hangs in the air over the city of Los Angeles. At the top of the steps, she fumbles for her key, and as she sets the bag down to get it from her purse, she sees a package propped against her front door. It is wrapped in brown paper, sent parcel post, and sealed with wide packing tape. It is the size of a shoebox.

Mirabelle uses her shoulder to jar open the front door, which has been sticking slightly from the week's rain. She puts the package on the kitchen table, double dips some dry cat food into a bowl, and checks her messages. She has none. She sits at the kitchen table and with a pair of scissors cuts off the package's dull outer wrapping. Inside is a pale red gift box, wrapped in an expensive white bow. She cuts the ribbon, opens the box, and sees a layer of tissue paper. There is a small note card on top, sealed in an envelope. She holds it up and studies the front, then turns it over and looks at the back. There are no revealing marks or brand names.

She parts the tissue, and inside is the pair of silver satin Dior gloves that she sold last Friday. She opens the note and reads, "I would like to have dinner with you." The bottom of the note is signed, Mr. Ray Porter.

She leaves the box on the kitchen table in a disarray of tissue. She backs out of the room and circulates nervously through the apartment, returning several times to the vicinity of the box. She doesn't touch it for the rest of the night, and she is afraid to move it because she does not understand it.

MONOTONY

Mirabelle's ambition is about one-tenth of 1 percent of what would be called normal. She has been at Neiman's almost two years without moving one inch forward. She considers herself an artist first, so her choice of jobs is immaterial. It doesn't matter to her if she is selling gloves or repainting apartments, as her real work is done in the evening with artists' crayon. Thus, she has zero ambition in these day jobs, and she tends to leave it to chance when it comes to getting and changing them. She is not aware that some people fight like alley cats for desirable situations. She presents a résumé, fills out an application, waits, and finally makes a call to see if she got the job. Usually, a confused secretary will answer and say that the position had been filled weeks ago. This aimlessness in presenting herself contributes to her feeling of being adrift.

She is, however, motivated to visit galleries and present her drawings to the dealer. She has established a relationship with a gallery on Melrose who will take a drawing and, six months later, sell it. But this does not produce enough outside income to set her free from being a shopgirl, and the inspiration required for a drawing exhausts her. And besides, she actually enjoys the monotony of Neiman's. In a way, when she is standing at the glove counter with her ankles crossed, she is perfect, and she likes the sense of accomplishment she gets from repetitive work.

So when she runs into Lisa at the Time Clock Café, she finds herself sitting across from her exact inverse. It is as though her every thought, trait, and belief had been turned inside out and decorated with a red wig. Lisa, idly curious about Mirabelle in the same way that a cat is curious about a dust mote, invites her to sit down. But Lisa's curiosity has talons, and she knows that in her approach to the glove girl, she must appear to be as benign as Mirabelle in order to casually extract the maximum information. If Immanuel Kant had stumbled across this luncheon after his noon Beverly Hills shrink appointment, he would have quickly discerned that Lisa is all phenomena and no noumena, and that Mirabelle is all noumena and no phenomena.

Mirabelle has a knack for discussing the mundane, at length. In this sense, she is Jeremy's blood brother. She can talk about glove storage nonstop. How her own ideas of storage are much better than the current system at Neiman's, and how her supervisor had become upset when he discovered that she had resorted them by size rather than color.

Today, she talks to Lisa about the intricacies of working at Neiman's, including the personality aberrations of her many bosses. This takes a while as practically everybody at Neiman's is her boss. These comments come from Mirabelle not as criticisms but as polite observations, and Lisa is confounded because she cannot discern an ulterior motive. Tom, the regular lunchtime Mirabelle-watcher, has spotted the two of them and is having his sandwich while trying to read their lips. He has also noted that Mirabelle's legs are slightly ajar, creating a wee wedge of a sight line right up her skirt. This keeps him at the lunch table a little longer than usual, ordering a dessert loaded with calories that he cannot afford. However, the periodic shifting of her legs creates a high anticipation in Tom that generates a compensating calorie-eating adrenaline. Suddenly, Lisa takes over with a breast-jutting arch of her back, and Tom's resulting caloric burn puts him back at even.

Mirabelle tells her about the mysterious glove delivery, mistakenly bringing Lisa into her inner circle of one. Lisa keeps an amused look on her face, but inside, this story sickens her, because it happened to someone else. Lisa can only think that this man's footpath had fallen just outside her orbit. She then gives Mirabelle advice that is so foreign to her that Mirabelle actually cannot comprehend it. The advice ranges from playing aloof, to looking up his credit card information, to returning the package unopened. The topic so excites Lisa that she forgets all her careful posturing with Mirabelle and blurts out her deepest and darkest:

"When a man approaches me, I know exactly what he wants. He wants to fuck me."

Mirabelle's back tenses and her legs reflexively close, prompting Tom to ask for his check.

"And if I like him, I fuck him a lot, until he gets addicted. Then I cut him off. That's when I've got him."

This is the extent, depth, and limit of Lisa's philosophy of life. Mirabelle stops midsip and stares at her as though looking at the first incoming pictures of an alien life form. She maneuvers the topic elsewhere, a few exchanges are made on other subjects, allowing Lisa to land on earth, and they finally split the check.

Lisa has taken all her intelligence and intuition, which is not meager, and focused a Cyclops eye on the soap operas of four square blocks of Beverly Hills, closing off her life. Mirabelle's outward-facing intelligence is gathering information, which is still coalescing and might not gel for several years. But she has always felt that her thirties were going to be her best decade, and since she is still lingering in her twenties, there is no hurry.

The rest of the day, and the next two days, rock to a lethargic syncopation. Moving too slowly to be counted by the clicks of a metronome, time is measured by lunches and closing times and customers, broken only by an occasional surge of curiosity about the intriguing package and her memory of the man who sent it. The mornings are sometimes busy, relatively, even producing a few sales in between the browsers, who generally scan the glove department as though they were looking into a stereoscope to view some antique photo. Mirabelle's brain activity, if it could be plotted by an electro-encephalogram, drops to a level that most scientists would interpret as sleep. On Thursday afternoon, she is brought back to life by an enthusiastic Japanese tourist who can't believe she has lucked upon the glove department, and who buys twelve pairs to be shipped back to Tokyo. This involves taking the address, calculating mailing costs, wrapping, and inscribing gift cards. The woman wants the Neiman's name on everything, including the gift cards, and Mirabelle calls around the store to find the old variety with the name embossed. In Mirabelle's world, this is the equivalent of running the three-minute mile and it leaves her worn out, complaining, and ready for an early night. Finally completing the last detail of the global transaction, she thanks the woman with the one foreign word that Neiman's requires its employees to know: *arigato.* The woman picks up her receipt, slips it in her shopping bag already crammed with previous purchases, cheerfully thanks Mirabelle with an engaging bow, and walks backward twelve steps until she turns and heads west toward couture. This is when Mirabelle becomes aware of a man standing to one side, who turns her with his voice. "So will you have dinner with me?" And then, because

Mirabelle doesn't reply, he says, "I'm Mr. Ray Porter."

"Oh," she says.

"I'm sorry if I was forward," he says, "but I'm practicing a new philosophy of life that involves being more forward."

While Mr. Ray Porter explains his presumption in sending her the gloves, Mirabelle sizes him up. Her intuition, rusty as it is, absorbs him in one single clinch, and no alarm bells sound. He is dressed for business – though without a tie – in a sharp blue suit. In every respect, size, height, weight, he is normal. Again, she checks out his shoes, and they are good. It is then she first notes, in the split second that has passed, that he is probably fifty years old.

Mirabelle forgets all about Lisa's complicated instructions and simply asks Mr. Ray Porter who he is. He tells her he lives in Seattle, but has a place in Los Angeles because he does business here. She asks if he is married and he says he is four years divorced. She asks if he has children and he says no. The question she does not ask, but is foremost in her mind, is "why me?" As these subtle negotiations proceed, it is determined that they will meet at a Beverly Hills Italian restaurant at 8 p.m. on Sunday. She declines to have him pick her up, and Mr. Ray Porter easily agrees. This keeps her free of all worries she might have about going to dinner with a total stranger: she can drive herself home. He has an easygoing manner that relaxes her, and they exchange exactly one semi-humorous line each. Both glance around to see if anyone is watching, and he seems to be aware that employees should not be seen chatting up customers, although vice versa is common. He backs away with an aside that he will need a map to find the glove department again, then he says something about how glad he is that she is coming to dinner, then he faintly blushes and disappears around a corner.

MR. RAY PORTER

There is nothing too mysterious about Ray Porter, at least in the usual sense of the word. He is single, he is kind, he tries to do the right thing, and he does not understand himself, or women, or his relationships with women. But there is one truth about him that can be said of a man who asks a woman to dinner before he has ever exchanged one personal word with her. Mr. Ray Porter is on the prowl. He does not know Mirabelle, he has only seen her. He has responded to something visceral, but that visceral thing is only in him, not between them. Not yet. He only imagines the character that unites her clothes, her skin, and her body. He has imagined the pleasure of touching her, and imagined her pleasure at being touched. She is a feminine object that tweaks him at his animal best.

Extrapolating from Mirabelle's wrist, he understands the terrain of her neck, he can imagine the valley of her breasts, and he knows that he can lose himself in her. He does not know his further intent with her, but he is not trying to get what he wants at any expense. If he thinks he would harm Mirabelle, he would back away. But he does not yet understand when and how people are hurt. He doesn't understand the subtleties of slights and pains, that it is not the big events that hurt the most but rather the smallest questionable shift in tone at the end of a spoken word that can plow most deeply into the heart. It seems to him that nothing in the world of relationships proves to be generally true, that nothing follows a logical sequence, and that his search for cohesion leaves him empty of answers.

His attraction to Mirabelle is not random. He is not out and about sending gloves all over the city. His action is a very spontaneous and specific response to something in her. It may have been her stance: at twenty yards she looks off-kilter and appealing. Or maybe it was her two pinpoint eyes that made her look innocent and vulnerable. Whatever it was, it started from an extremely small place that Mr. Ray Porter never could have identified, even under torture.

His small house and furnishings in the Hollywood Hills tell one simple story; Mr. Ray Porter has money. Enough that there is never a problem, any time or any place. The giveaway is the lighting. Little hidden spotlights alternate with warm lamplight, creating a soft yellow glow that implies "decorator." The house, being a second home used for business only, isn't strewn with personal objects. It is this anonymous quality, like being on vacation in an expensive hotel room, that makes you want to take off your clothes and start fucking. In the bedroom, there is a fireplace opposite an antique four-poster bed, with books piled high on either side, all nonfiction and all stuck with three or four bookmarks. The house focuses on the view of the city that Mirabelle is so casually denied.

Neatness, which the house displays on every coffee table and bathroom countertop, is not a characteristic of Ray Porter. Neatness is a quality that he admires, however, and therefore buys, by hiring an obsessive maid.

In the garage are two cars. One is a gray Mercedes, the other a gray Mercedes. The second gray Mercedes is used for hauling his sports equipment, so he won't have to load and unload every time he feels like a bike ride. A rack hangs incongruously on the back, and in the trunk are rollerblades and a tennis racquet. When Mr. Ray Porter tempts fate by exercising in traffic, he wears a twenty-first-century version of armor, which offers similar protection but not the romance: a beaked plastic bicycle helmet, elbow pads, and knee pads. He dons this getup whether it is winter or summer, meaning for three months out of the year he wears large black knee pads while wearing shorts. When he is astride his bicycle, tooling down a Seattle main street and sporting this outfit, the only visible difference between Ray Porter and an insect is his size.

The kitchen is the most unused part of the house. Since his divorce, the kitchen has become like a middle-American living room: for display only. Usually he eats out, alone, or tries to fill the evening with friends or a date. These dinner dates, which function mainly to fill a vacuum of loneliness between the hours of 8 p.m. and 11 p.m., cause him more grief than a year of solitary confinement. For even though they look like dates and sound like dates, and sometimes result in a liaison, to him they aren't exactly dates. They are friendly evenings that sometimes end in bed. He incorrectly assumes that whatever is his understanding of the nature of one of these evenings, his date is thinking it, too, and he is deeply shocked and surprised when one or another of these women, whom he has seen over the past several months and with whom he has had several sexual encounters, actually believes they are a couple.

These experiences have caused him to think very hard about what he is doing and where he is going. And the result of all this thinking is that he now understands that he doesn't know what he is doing or where he is going. His professional life is fine, but romantically he is an adolescent, and he has begun an education in the subject that is thirty years overdue.

His interest in Mirabelle comes from the part of him that still believes he can have her without obligation. He believes he can exist with her from eight to eleven and enter a private and personal world that they will create that will cease to exist in the off hours or off days. He believes that this world will be independent of other worlds he might create on another night, in another place, and he has no intention of allowing it to affect his true quest for a mate. He believes that in this affair, what is given back and forth will be exactly even, and that they will both see the benefits they are receiving. But because he picked Mirabelle out by sight alone, he fails to see that her fragility, which he smelled and sensed and is lured by, runs deep in her heart and is part of her nature, and cannot be separated out for him to fuck.

௭

Ray and Mirabelle have similar ideas about wardrobe. He likes a stylish look, though modified for his age. He has lots of suits in striking fabrics, and his money enables him to make mistakes and get rid of them. His closet has his L.A. clothes, which means he can travel to and from Seattle with no suitcase. The drawback to this arrangement is that he will arrive at his home, see a shirt he hasn't worn for three months because he has been out of town, and feel like he is slipping into a new look. His L.A. friends have an entirely different view. They see that he is wearing exactly the same shirt he wore last time.

His aversion to carrying luggage, eventually causing him to buy a house in L.A. so he could stock it with clothes, comes from a mildly obsessive belief in the management of his time. Standing at a baggage carousel, being jostled by passengers while scanning a hundred similar bags for a number to match his claim check, which is always misplaced, does not sit well with his logic. He has no time to be exasperated, especially if he can solve it by buying a house. This need for efficiency dictates many of his daily movements. In setting out his breakfast, he will accomplish all the tasks that occur on one side of the kitchen before starting the tasks that originate on the other side of the kitchen. He will never cross to the refrigerator for orange juice, cross back to the cabinet to get cereal, and cross back again to the refrigerator for milk. This behavior is rooted in a subterranean logic a robot programmed for efficiency might display.

Luckily, this behavior is not entirely fixed in him. It escalates during busy times and wanes during evenings and vacations. However, it translates itself into other forms so removed from the original impulse as to be unrecognizable. His attraction to Mirabelle is an abstraction of this behavior: her cleanliness and simplicity represent an economy that other women do not have.

Ray Porter parks the car and enters the house in his most efficient way. The garage door is closed by remote control while he is still in the car gathering his papers. This saves him pausing at the kitchen door to press the indoor remote.

Tp 3,

his little abbreviation is second nature to him. Once inside, he sets his papers down in the kitchen, even though they need to be in his office. He will take them later when he has to go to the office via the kitchen. There is no point taking them to the office now, as he needs to beeline to the living room to make reservations for Sunday.

He sits on the sofa, turns on the TV news, starts reading the newspaper, and simultaneously starts dialing the restaurant. He makes reservations at a small but sweet place in Beverly Hills that is on his speed dial. La Ronde, an Italian restaurant with a French name (the culinary complement to Rodeo Drive's French chateaus with Italian porticos tacked on), offers quiet and privacy to an older man who walks in with a twenty-eight-year-old who looks twenty-four. Then, after attending to the TV and browsing the newspaper until he is absolutely bored, he begins to do what he does best. He raises his head toward the view, which by now has transformed into sparkling white dots of light set in black velvet, and begins to think. What goes through his head are streams of logical chains, computer code, if-then situations, complicated mathematical structures, words, non sequiturs. Usually, these chains will unravel into loose ends or pointless conclusions; sometimes they will form something concrete, which he can sell. This ability to focus absolutely has brought him millions of dollars, and why this is so can never be explained to normal people, except to say that the source of his money is embedded deeply in a software string so fundamental that to change it now would be to reorganize the entire world. He is not filthy rich; his contribution is just a tiny line of early code that he had copyrighted, and that they had needed.

Tonight, these mental excursions get him nowhere and finally he gets on the phone to a Seattle girlfriend, or as he really thinks of it, a woman in Seattle who is a friend he is having sex with who is fully informed that they are never going to be a couple. "Hey." "Hey," she says back. "What're you doin'?" she says. "Staring at my knees. Nothing much. You okay?" She replies, "Yeah." He senses she's upset over something and digs deeper. She responds by spilling out her woes – mostly work related – and he listens attentively, like John Gray in a nest of divorcées. The conversation finally runs out of gas. "Well, this is good, this is a good talk. So I'll see you when I get back. By the way, I think I should tell you I have a date on Sunday. Thought I should let you know." "All right, all right," she counters, "you don't have to tell me everything, you just don't, just keep it to yourself." "Shouldn't I tell you, though?" he replies. "Shouldn't I?"

She tries to explain, but can't. He tries to understand her, but can't. He knows this is an area where logic doesn't apply and he just listens and learns the lesson for next time.

This information, this anecdotal training in the understanding of women, gleaned from experience, books, advice, and mostly hurt feelings being hurled at him, fits in no previous compartment of his experience, and he has created a new memory bank just for housing it all. This memory bank is in a jumble. It is not coherent. Occasionally his more rational mind will venture in and try to arrange it, like a boy cleaning his room. But just when everything is in its place, the metaphor holds and two days later the room is a mess.

These encounters are probably the most formative experiences of his early fifties. He is collecting pleasures and pains, gathered from his relationships with ballerinas and librarians, decent females without the right pheromones, and nut-balls. He is like a child learning what is too hot to touch, and he hopes all this experience will coalesce into a philosophy of life, or at least a philosophy of relationships, that will transform itself into instinct. This fact-finding mission, in the guise of philandering, is necessary because as a youth he failed to observe women properly. He never sorted them into types, or catalogued their neuroses so he could spot them again from the tiniest clue. He is now taking a remedial course in fucking 101, to learn how to handle the diatribes, inexplicable antics, insults, and misunderstandings that seem to him to be the inevitable conclusion to the syllogism of sex. But he is not aware that he is on such a serious mission: he thinks he is a bachelor having a good time.

That night, he calls a restaurant that delivers and he orders an appropriate meal for a fifty-year-old. This is easier in L.A. than in Seattle, as most take-out food in any part of the country involves fat and cholesterol. In L.A., however, it's a snap to order a low-fat veggie burger, or sushi, delivered right to your door no matter how complicated the route to your house. In Los Angeles you can live in the tiniest apartment in the tiniest cul de sac with a 1/4 in your address and twenty minutes after placing an order a foreigner will knock on your door bearing yam fries and meatless meatloaf. And if Ray's solitary dinner at home were broadcast on satellite, the world would learn that millionaires, too, eat their dinners out of a white paper bag while standing in the kitchen. Even Mirabelle knows not to do that, as the self-prepared dinner is a great time killer for lonely people, and as much time should be spent on it as possible.

After the food arrives via the smallest car he has ever seen, Ray Porter turns on a small TV in the kitchen and begins channel flipping. At that moment he becomes Jeremy's soul mate; their two hearts beat as one as they eat from a sack and rapidly click their way through the entire broadcast range, with similar timing of the occasional paper rustle and periodic foot shift. They are nearly indistinguishable as they engage in this rite, except that one man stands in the kitchen of a two-million-dollar house overlooking the city, and the other in a one-room garage apartment that the city overlooked. If Mr. Ray Porter knew where to train his telescope, he might even have been able to peer down fifteen miles to Silverlake, right into Jeremy's window, and if Jeremy weren't in an impenetrable stupor, he might even have been able to wave back. And if three lines were drawn, joining the homes of Jeremy and Ray to Mirabelle's wobbly flat, the apex of the triangle would pinpoint the unlikely connection between these two wildly opposite men.

Mr. Ray Porter gets into bed and closes his eyes. He visualizes Mirabelle sitting on his chest, wearing the same simple orange cotton skirt she wore on the day he first saw her. He imagines the skirt draped over his head, so he can see her legs, her stomach, and her white cotton underwear. The lamplight penetrates the skirt and casts an orange glow over everything in his little imaginary tent. A sunset of flesh and fabric, which sends him into an onanistic fit. He is then silent and satiated, with a ghostly image of Mirabelle still lingering in his head. But soon an arbitrary array of untethered words, logical marks, and symbols rushes through his mind, sweeping away everything. Minutes later, his mind is clear and he falls asleep.

DATE

Mirabelle's first dilemma is the valet parker. She can't afford to pay someone three-fifty plus tip to whisk her car away. But parking is restricted and she will have to leave her car several blocks away if she doesn't. She decides it is inelegant to arrive on this first date looking windblown, and she slides the car to the curb and takes the check the valet hands her, praying that Mr. Ray Porter will take pity on someone who is currently carrying only eight dollars in cash. The car vanishes and she pulls on the restaurant door but it won't open, then she pushes, then realizes she is trying to open the hinged side, then she pushes on the correct side, then pulls, and the door finally gives way. She enters a darkened little cave, certainly not the hip spot in town, and sees a jury of older diners wearing gold-buttoned blazers and big shirt collars. There is a saving grace, though. A young actor from a hot television show, Trey Bryan, sits in the corner with several producer types, and his presence saves the place from being complete squaresville. The maître d', a once dashing

Italian, approaches her with a "Buona sera," and Mirabelle wonders what he said.

"I'm meeting Mr. Ray Porter," she chances.

"Ah. Nice to see you again. Right this way."

He leads Mirabelle past several red leather banquettes and around a lattice. In a booth too large for two people sits Ray Porter. He is looking down at a notepad and doesn't see her at first, but he looks up almost immediately. The incandescent lighting, filtered through the red lampshades, warms everybody up, and to him, she looks better than at Neiman's. He rises to greet her and guides her into the booth, and sits her to his right.

"Do you remember my name?" he asks.

"Yes, and all the exciting times we've had."

"Would you like a drink?"

"Red wine?" she questions.

"Do you like Italian?"

"I'm not sure what I like; I'm still forming," says Mirabelle.

Ray Porter is relieved that he can desire her and like her at the same time. The waiter attends them and Ray orders two glasses of Barolo from the wine list, as Mirabelle plays with her spoon.

"So why did you go out with me?" He cascades his napkin open and lays it on his lap.

"I think that's an impolite question." Mirabelle puts the right amount of coy in her voice.

"Fair enough," says Ray Porter.

"So why did you ask me out?" says Mirabelle.

The fundamentally simple answer to that question is rarely spoken on any first date ever. And the real answer doesn't occur to Ray, Mirabelle, or even the waiter. Fortunately Ray Porter has a logical reply that prevents a silence that would have been awkward for both of them.

"If it's impolite for me, it's impolite for you."

"Fair enough," says Mirabelle.

"Fair enough," says Ray Porter.

And they sit, each in a tiny struggle about what to say next. Finally, Mirabelle succeeds.

"How did you get my address?" she says.

"Sorry about that. I just did, that's all. I lied to Neiman's and got your last name, then one call to information."

"Have you done that before?

"I think I've done everything before. But no, I don't think I've done that before."

"Thank you for the gloves."

"Do you have anything to wear them with?"

"Yes, plaid shorts and sneakers."

He looks at her, then realizes she has made a joke.

"What do you do?" he asks.

"What do you mean?"

"I mean besides work at Neiman's?"

"I'm an artist. I draw. I can draw."

"I can't draw a line. A sheet of paper is less valuable once I've scribbled on it. What do you draw?"

"Usually dead things."

At this point, Ray Porter imagines an entirely different iceberg beneath Mirabelle's psychic waterline than the one that actually exists.

The wine arrives. The waiter pours it as they sit in silence. When he leaves, they speak again.

She asks him about himself and Mr. Ray Porter tells her, all the while his eyes drifting down the line of her neck to her white starched blouse, which, as she breathes, bellows open and closed. This half inch of space allows him a view of her skin, just above her breasts, which nestles into the white of her bra. He wants to poke his hand in and leave a light, pale fingerprint on her. His glances toward her take place between Mirabelle's own glances toward him, so that these looks to each other are effectively woven together, yet never intercepted by either.

They make it through to the end of the evening, with the conversation lasting just until the check comes, at which point they run out of topics. Then they deal with the business part of the evening, that part where phone numbers are exchanged and hours indicated when it is best to call. Ray Porter gives her his Seattle number as well, the direct line, not the office. As they leave the restaurant, he places his hand on the small of her back in a gesture of assistance as she passes through the door. This is their absolute first physical contact and does not go unnoticed by either's subconscious.

Mirabelle's car comes first, and she troops around to

the open door, where she begins to fumble in her purse for a tip. "It's been taken care of," says the valet.

She drives home, not sure of what she is feeling, but filled with what is probably the first truly expensive meal of her life. When she gets home, there is a message from Ray Porter asking her to dinner next Thursday. There is also a message from Jeremy asking her to call him back, that night. Her responsibility gene kicks in, and she phones him, even though it is twenty-five minutes short of midnight.

"Yeah?" Jeremy believes this is a clever way to answer the phone.

"You wanted me to call?" says Mirabelle.

"Yeah. Thanks. Oh, hi. What are you doing?"

"You mean now?"

"Yeah, wanna come over?" says Jeremy.

Mirabelle thinks of Lisa. She wonders how he can be addicted so soon. They hardly did it and she hardly cut it off. One sloppy evening of flaccid sex and Jeremy is begging for another soggy dog biscuit. Lisa's phone must be ringing off the hook. She must have endless messages of coercion on her machine from sad-eyed lovers.

"Come on over," continues Jeremy.

This inquiry reverses every electron in Mirabelle's body, causing her attraction to Jeremy, which was at one time a weak North-South, to become a strong North-North. It is the perfect wrong time for Jeremy to do to Mirabelle what she had done to him – call him up for a quick fix – because, in a sense, she is now betrothed. Her first date with someone who treated her well obligates her to faithfulness, at least until the relationship is explored. She does not want to betray this unspoken promise to Ray Porter. But Mirabelle is polite, even when she doesn't have to be, and she thinks she owes Jeremy at least a conversation. After all, he wasn't so awful, and she continues:

"It's too late," she says.

"It's not too late," he counters.

"It's too late for me. I have to get up."

"Come on."

"I can't."

"Come on."

"No."

"It's not too late."

"No."

"Want me to come over there?"

"It's too late."

"I can be over there in ten minutes."

"No."

"Wanna meet somewhere?"

"I can't."

"We could meet somewhere."

"I have to hang up."

"I could come over and then leave early so you could sleep."

Mirabelle convinces Jeremy that no way, not now, not tonight, not ever, is he getting her in bed when it isn't her idea, and finally she gets him off the phone. This incident has sullied the events of the evening, and she has to concentrate to get herself back to her earlier buzz.

She putters around the kitchen, remembering this or that about her dinner with Ray Porter, also noting that this was one of the first evenings in a long time that hadn't cost her anything. She is pleased that she had been her best self, that she had entered a new world and had been comfortable in it. She had given something back to the person who took her out. She had made jokes, she had been wry, she had been pretty for him. She had turned him on. She had listened. And in return, he had put his hand on the small of her back and paid for her parking and bought her dinner. To Mirabelle this exchange seems fair and good, and next time, if he asks, she will kiss him.

Ray Porter's faithfulness ratio is somewhat different. While he also had a good time, meaning that the evening was charged with little invisible ions of attraction, this does not mean that any devotion is in order at all. What it does mean is that they will have several or many dates, and until something is indicated or promised otherwise, they are independent of each other. But this is such a routine thought for Ray Porter that he doesn't even bother to think it. He had called her from his car phone with an invitation for Thursday not only because he liked her but also because there is a riddle in his mind. Upon reflection, he cannot tell if the surface he glimpsed under Mirabelle's blouse was her skin or a flesh-colored nylon underthing. As he weighs the evidence, he decides that it had to be a nylon underthing as what he saw was too uniform, too perfect, too balanced in color to be skin. On the other hand, if it was her skin, then she possesses his particular intoxicant, a heady milk bath he can submerge himself in, and soak in, and drown in. He knows that this riddle will probably not be solved on Thursday, but without it, there will be no Saturday, which is the next logical step in its solution.

He gets in bed, and instead of letting the streams of data pour through his mind, he lets the symbols of sex form their own strict logic. The white blouse implies the skin which implies the bra which implies her breasts which implies her neck and her hair. This leads to her stomach which necessarily invokes her abdomen which leads to her inner thigh which leads to her panties which leads to a damp line on white cotton that he can press on and gain a millimeter of access to her vagina. This access leads to further access and implies taste and aroma and a unification of his self made possible by the possession of his very opposite. This logical sequence is plotted against a series of intermittent days that spread over several months. The entire formula is a function of whether the square inch in question is skin or nylon, and if it is nylon, what then is the true texture of the square inch hidden beneath it?

GLOVES

Mirabelle strides confidently past the working stiffs on the first floor and heads to her sanctuary on the fourth. She takes the stairs two steps at a time, and oddly, she is in the mood to work. She is even thinking of ways to sell more gloves by laying a few out on the end tables and display cases throughout the store. Then she gets to her department, takes her post, crosses her legs at the ankles, and stands there. And stands there. No management comes by all day for her to spill her idea to. There is more for her to look at, however, as the pre-Thanksgiving nonrush means more people pass by her counter on their way to somewhere else. Lunchtime comes, and she has a definite feeling that she has not moved for three and a half hours.

She decides to take a two-hour lunch. This is accomplished through lying. She explains to her immediate boss, Mr. Agasa, that she has an appointment for a female problem and that she tried to schedule it for another time but that this is the only time the doctor can take her. Mr. Agasa stammers while she adds that things are slow and that she has asked Lisa to keep an eye on the counter, and he nods a concerned okay.

"Are you all right?" he asks.

"I think I'm okay, but I should be checked."

And she leaves the store. Hitting the flats of Beverly Hills, she pops into a yogurt shop on the premise that she can have an entire meal for three dollars, and she takes her brimming cup outside and vacations in the sun on Bedford Drive. In the hard sunlight, her hair shines a deep maroon. She angles her wire chair toward the low-rise that houses all the Beverly Hills shrinks, hoping to spot a few celebrities. This is the building where she goes to renew her medication, so she recognizes a few of the nurses and receptionists who file in and out. Next to her sits a woman so repulsive that Mirabelle has to turn her body uncomfortably so as to edge her out of her peripheral vision. The woman converses on a cell phone while shoveling in contradictory amounts of low-calorie yogurt. Her fat droops over the chair and hides all but its legs. Her hair is brassy from chemicals designed to make it look golden, and her smoker's face has a subtle gray cast. However, what she speaks about on the phone is in fact quite gentle. She is concerned about someone who is ill, which makes Mirabelle squirm a little over her lie to Mr. Agasa. The woman speaks, stops, then after what must have been a long speech by the person on the other end of the line, says,

" . . . just remember, darling, it is pain that changes our lives."

Mirabelle cannot fathom the meaning of this sentence, as she has been in pain her whole life, and yet it remains unchanged.

Just then she sees the heartthrob Trey Bryan enter the shrinks' building. Trey Bryan is hot as a pistol, which qualifies him for immediate psychoanalytic care. She had seen him once in Neiman's buying what looked very much like doilies for his girlfriend's shoulders. She has witnessed heartthrob shopping many times, and she knows it is a ritual that is very refined. It requires a girlfriend who, if not already famous, is comfortable with becoming famous. She has to look bored, and therein lies the purpose of the shopping trip: the heartthrob must dance around laying gifts at her feet, trying to lift her spirits. Mirabelle could never figure out why the receiver of these gifts is so bored. Mirabelle loves to get gifts.

An important part of the celebrity-couple shopping ritual is that the two shoppers appear exclusive; their world is so extraordinary, so charged, that their movement through the regular, unexclusive world scatters little dewdrops of diamonds. Mirabelle had once waited on such a couple, when she stood in at the Comme des Garcons section, and felt her own transparency. It was as though she were a chalk outline of herself, animated by an inferior life force.

Today, though, with her extra hour and fifteen minutes, and the sun beating down on her in spite of it being November, she decides to visit the competition and check out the glove departments at a few other stores. She can at least empathize with other sad, lost girls who stand in solitude behind their counters. Her first stop is Saks Fifth Avenue on Wilshire Boulevard, where she sees an impression of herself standing vacantly in the lonely distance, hovering over merchandise that no one wants. She says her name and identifies herself by job description, and the clerk is so excited to have someone talking to her that Mirabelle considers offering her a Serzone to level her out.

Next stop is Theodore on Rodeo Drive. This is a hip, sexy store and features gloves so youthful and spirited that Mirabelle longs to deal in them. She can imagine the coolest people coming to her, swapping fashion tips as they try on the merchandise. To take advice from her current customers would be fashion suicide, unless she somehow wanted to be mistaken for fifty.

As she drifts around Beverly Hills, she finds herself a block from La Ronde. This arouses no particular emotional response, it is not "the place where they rendezvoused," but it does make her feel less like an outsider in Beverly Hills. She has actually eaten in one of the actual restaurants, which is what 90 percent of the out-of-towners roaming around this afternoon haven't done. She wanders into the Pay-Less and buys sanitary napkins, because she needs some, and because it will reinforce her lie to Mr. Agasa should he see her purchase.

She goes back to Neiman's, where Lisa tells her that

someone has been looking for her. "Who?" asks Mirabelle.

"Well, I don't know, a man."

Mirabelle assumes it is Ray Porter. Perhaps canceling. She will call her message machine at her first break.

"What was he like?" Mirabelle asks Lisa.

"He's a man, over fifty. Normal."

"What else?"

"A little overweight. And he asked for Mirabelle Buttersfield. By name."

Ray Porter is not overweight and would not ask for Mirabelle by her last name, which she is not even sure he knows.

"He said he'll come back," adds Lisa, vanishing toward the stairwell.

Mirabelle slides back into her berth behind the counter. She stands there a minute and is suddenly struck by an overwhelming wave of sadness. This causes her to do something she has never done at Neiman's: she pulls out a low drawer in the counter and sits on it for several minutes, until she recovers.

LISA

Lisa Cramer's body is good enough for any man or woman on this planet, but it is not good enough for Lisa Cramer. She believes that she has to be flawlessly pleasing to a man, and that she has to be an expert at fellatio. This talent is fine-tuned and polished through extensive conversations with other women and the viewing of selected "educational" porno tapes. She even once attended a class given by Crystal Headly, a down and going sex-film actress. She is not reluctant to roll out this expertise, either. Within several dates, and sometimes sooner, Lisa will demonstrate this skill to the lucky fella, thus making herself feel that she is the kind of woman any man would want. The men, however, feel confounded by their good fortune. Who is this person who goes down on them so easily? Lisa can only judge her success by the frequency of follow-up phone calls from the men, who are eager to take her to dinner, or a play. The fact that they are willing to take her to a play – low on the list of L.A. date priorities – demonstrates just how far they are willing to go. Lisa knows it is the sex they are after, but it is sex that is the source of her worth. The more they want it, the more valuable she is, and consequently, Lisa has made herself into a fuckable object.

Lisa is not interested in sex because it is fun. It is the fulcrum and lever for attracting and discarding men. They come to her because of a high hope, an aroma that she gives off, as delicious as baking bread. But when she's done with them, they are limp and drained, and ready for their own bed. She has literally absorbed all their interest, and she wants them to retreat before they discover some horrible flaw in her that will repulse them. Thus Lisa, with all her power, never feels quite good enough for anything beyond her ability to create desire in men. In fact, several prohibitive compulsions appeared in her early twenties that keep her from widening her circle of experience. She cannot get on an airplane. Fear of flying grips her so intensely that she has forever banished air travel as a possibility. She also cannot ingest any medicine of any kind. Not aspirin, not antibiotics, not even a Tums, for fear of losing her mind. And she can never, ever, be alone, without worrying that she will suddenly die.

Lisa has developed a taste for Mr. Ray Porter, even though she has never met him. There is simply a problem that he has selected Mirabelle and not her as his arbitrary object of desire, and Lisa is sure that once he lays eyes on her, correct thinking will occur. Lisa cannot imagine Mirabelle being an expert sex partner. Of course, Mirabelle's lack of advanced training might be exactly why Ray Porter wants her, but this reasoning is way beyond Lisa, because she has no idea that her own sovereignty could be usurped by one square inch of Mirabelle's skin, glimpsed under a starched blouse.

The day Lisa heard Mirabelle blab her story at the Time Clock, a vestigial memory was jarred in her head at the mention of the name Ray Porter. Lisa went home that night, concentrated, and remembered that his name had been in the air a few years ago because he had picked up and had an affair with a shoe clerk at Barneys, the fashionable department store two doors down. Then, when he came in with another woman six months after the affair was over, the salesgirl went berserk and threw two pairs of Stephane Kelian shoes at him, with one falling into an open fish tank, and she was promptly fired. Barneys has a "don't ask don't tell" policy when it comes to customers and employees, and throwing shoes clearly violates the "don't tell." Lisa also remembers that Ray Porter is powerful.

Lisa doesn't see an interposition of herself between Mirabelle and Ray Porter as unethical. In her mind, Mirabelle deserves no one, and Lisa will be doing him a favor. What would Ray Porter do with a leaden Mirabelle lying nude on his bed with her legs open? What would any man do with a soggy girl who can't assert herself, who has a weak voice, who dresses like a schoolgirl, and whose main personality component is helplessness?

SECOND DATE

Before Thursday's date, there are several formal phone conversations between Ray and Mirabelle, which establish that he will pick her up, that the time will be 8 p.m., and that they will go to a fun local Caribbean spot that Mirabelle knows called Cha Cha Cha. She is concerned about him seeing her apartment, which, at five hundred dollars a month, is only slightly more than the cost of their meal at La Ronde. She is also concerned that he'll have trouble finding it. The apartment is at the conjunction of a maze of streets in Silverlake, and once found, still requires complicated directions to achieve the door. Down the driveway, second stairway, around the landing . . . .

When Thursday comes, Mirabelle speed cleans the apartment while simultaneously dusting herself with powders and pulling various dresses over her head. She settles on a short pink and yellow plaid skirt and a fuzzy pink sweater, which sadly prohibits any of Ray's peeking. This outfit, in combination with her cropped hair, makes her look about nineteen. This look is not meant to appeal to something lascivious in Ray but is worn as a hip mode-o-day that will fit right in at Cha Cha Cha.

Then, finally prepared, she sits in her living room and waits. Mirabelle doesn't have a real sofa, only a low-lying futon cradled in a wood brace, which means that anyone attempting to sit on it is immediately jackknifed at floor level. If a visitor allows an arm to fall to one side, it will land on the gritty hardwood. If he sits with a drink, it has to be put on the floor at cat level. She reminds herself not to ask Ray to sit down.

The phone rings. It is Ray, calling from his car phone, saying he is only a little bit lost. She gives him the proper lefts and rights, and within five minutes, he is knocking at her door. She answers, and both of them scurry in to avoid the harsh glare of the bare hundred-watt porch bulb.

If Mirabelle worried about Ray seeing her apartment, her concern was misplaced. This collegiate atmosphere dislodges a musty erotic memory in him, and he feels a few vague waves of pleasure coursing just below his skin. Mirabelle asks him if he wants anything, knowing that she has nothing to give him except canned clam juice. He declines, but wants to snoop around the apartment, and he pokes his nose into the kitchen, where he sees the college-girl dish rack and the college-girl mismatched drinking glasses and the college-girl cat box. The problem, of course, is that Mirabelle is already four years out of college and has not been able to earn an income at the next level.

She asks him if he wants to sit down, which she immediately regrets, and Ray squats down onto the futon, bending himself into a crouch that for someone over fifty would be considered an advanced yoga position. After the absolute minimum conversation required to make the futon invitation not ridiculous, she suggests they leave. As Ray helps himself up, his body sounds a few audible creaks.

They leave the apartment and walk toward his Mercedes, with all the spontaneity of a prom date. Driving, he stiffly points out the features of the car, including the electric seat warmers, which prompt a few jokes from both of them. At the restaurant, they squirm and talk and wriggle until midway through the entrée, which is a chili-hot fish of some kind prepared to blast the heads off all comers. Things are wooden between them, and would have remained so for the complicated second date, had it not been for an elixir called Bordeaux.

The wine greases things up a bit, and this little relaxation, this gear slippage, makes Ray bold enough to touch her wrist. He says he likes her watch. It isn't much, but it is a beginning. Mirabelle knows that her watch is of a dullness that could arouse no opinion at all, and even though her own eyes have filled with shallow pools of alcohol, she suspects that this contact is not about her watch but about Ray's desire to touch her. And she's right. For as Ray drags the tip of his finger across the back of her hand, he measures the degree of tropical humidity that her skin delivers to his fingertip, and impulses of pleasure leap from neuron to neuron and are delivered to his receptive brain.

He slips his finger and thumb around her wrist. "Now I'm your watch," he says, boyishly. Mirabelle and Ray, not drunk but hovering, are trying to figure some way out of the conversational mess they have gotten themselves in. Ray really wants to be driving around with his hand on her thigh, but he is stuck here in Cha Cha Cha making small talk. Mirabelle wants them to be strolling down Silverlake Boulevard holding hands, getting to know each other, but she needs a closing line about the watch, or they are just going to languish forever in endless circularity. Then Ray has a brilliant idea. He orders one more glass of wine and suggests they both drink from the same glass. Mirabelle is not a drinker, so Ray downs about two-thirds of it, and right in front of her gets out a pen and calculates his body weight versus the amount drunk minus the food eaten, and announces he is okay to drive. Which leads them to the car.

Which leads them to her porch.

Where he kisses her good night, and presses himself against her, and she feels him thicken against her legs. And neither cares about the harsh porch light. And he says good night. And as he walks away, he thinks that he cannot imagine anything better than their next date.

THEIR NEXT DATE

Mirabelle ends up at Ray's house, where, fully clothed, they get on his bed and she sits on top of him and he unbuttons three buttons on her blouse and he finds the area above her breasts and confirms that it is her skin he had seen at La Ronde and not a flesh-colored underthing. That's all they do, and he drives her home.

THE CONVERSATION

The Conversation consists of one involved party telling another involved party the limits of their interest. It is meant to be a warning to the second party that they may come only so close.

Again, Mr. Ray Porter takes Mirabelle to La Ronde. They sit at the same booth and have the same wine, and everything is done to replicate their first dinner, because Ray wants to pick up exactly where they left off, with not even a design change in a fork handle to break the continuum. Mirabelle is not sparkling tonight, because she works only in gears, and tonight she is in the wrong gear. Third gear is her scholarly, perspicacious, witty self; second gear is her happy, giddy, childish self; and first gear is her complaining, helpless, unmotivated self. Tonight she is somewhere midshift, between helpless and childish, but Ray doesn't care. Ray doesn't care because tonight is the night as far as he is concerned, the night where everything is going to come off her. And Ray feels compelled to have the Conversation. It is appropriate tonight because of Ray's fairness doctrine:

before the clothes come off, speeches must be made.

"I think I should tell you a few things. I don't think I'm ready for a real relationship right now." He says this not to Mirabelle but to the air, as though he is just discovering a truth about himself and accidentally speaking it aloud.

Mirabelle answers, "You had a rough time with your divorce."

Understanding. For Ray Porter, that is good. She absolutely knows that this will never be long term. He goes on: "But I love seeing you and I want to keep seeing you."

"I do too," says Mirabelle. Mirabelle believes he has told her that he is bordering on falling in love with her, and Ray believes she understands that he isn't going to be anybody's boyfriend.

"I'm traveling too much right now," he says. In this sentence, he serves notice that he would like to come into town, sleep with her, and leave. Mirabelle believes that he is expressing frustration at having to leave town and that he is trying to cut down on traveling.

"So what I'm saying is that we should be allowed to keep our options open, if that's okay with you."

At this point, Ray believes he has told her that in spite of what could be about to happen tonight, they are still going to see other people. Mirabelle believes that after he cuts down on his traveling, they will see if they should get married or just go steady.

So now they have had the Conversation. What neither

of them understands is that these conversations are meaningless. They are meaningless to the sayer and they are meaningless to the hearer. The sayer believes they are heard, and the hearer believes they are never said. Men, women, dogs, and cats, these words are never heard.

They chat through dinner, and then Ray asks her if she would like to come to his house, and she says yes.

SEXUAL INTERCOURSE

With one switch, the lighting in Ray's house goes from post office to jazz nightclub. He starts fantasizing about events that are only moments away. His hours of being with Mirabelle and not having her are about to give way to unrestricted passage. The memory of her sitting on top of him, when he gave a slight squeeze of her breasts through layers of clothing, crystallizes his desire and causes it to crackle.

Ray is lured on not simply because he is a guy and she is a girl. It is just that Mirabelle's body, as he will soon discover, is his absolute aphrodisiac. His intuition sensed it, led him to the fourth floor, and has been reinforced with every whiff and accidental touch. He deduced it from the sight of her, and from the density of her hair and the length of her fingers, and from the phosphorus underglow of her skin. And tonight, he will feel the beginning of an addiction that he cannot break, the endless push and pull of an intoxication that he suspects he should avoid but cannot resist.

He puts both hands on the sides of her neck, but she

stiffens. She says it makes her nervous. This takes a bit of undoing, and he breaks from her, makes a few irrelevant comments, and resumes. They get on the bed and dally, a mesh of buttons and buckles and shoes clashing and gnashing. This time he buries his face in her neck and draws in his breath, inhaling her natural perfume. This gets the appropriate response. A few clothes are removed.

They are relaxed. They are not on a straight path to intercourse, as they take talking breaks, joking breaks, adjusting-the-music breaks. Things intensify, then ebb, then reheat. After a few minutes with Ray exploring the landscape of her bare stomach, he takes a bathroom break and disappears through a doorway.

Mirabelle stands up and methodically takes off all her clothes. Then she lies face down on the bed and smiles to herself. Because Mirabelle knows she is revealing her most secret and singular asset.

Mirabelle's body is not extravagant. It does not flirt, or call out, and that causes men who care about drama to shop elsewhere. But, when viewed at the radius of a king-sized bed, or held in the hands, or manipulated for pleasure, it is a small spectacle of perfection.

Ray enters the bedroom and sees her. Her skin looks like it has faint micro lights under it, glowing from rose to white. Her breasts peek out from her sides as they are flattened against the sheets, and the line of her body rises and falls in gentle waves. He walks over and puts his hand on her lower back, lingers there, then rolls her over, kisses her neck, runs his hand down her legs and in between, then touches her breasts, then kisses her mouth while he cups her vagina until it opens, then he eats her, makes love to her, as safely as the moment allows. Again she thinks how different this is from Vermont. Then he faces her away from him and brings his body up next to hers. Mirabelle, fetal, curled up like a bug, receives the proximity of Ray Porter as though it were a nourishing stream. They wake in the morning on either side of the bed.

BREAKFAST

At breakfast, early because she has to get to work, Mirabelle becomes age seven. She sits, waiting to be served. Ray Porter gets the juice, makes the coffee, sets the plates, toasts the bread, and pours the cereal. He gets the paper. Mirabelle is so dependent, she could have used a nanny to hold open her mouth and spoon-feed her the oat bran. She speaks in one-word sentences, which requires Ray to fill the silences with innocuous queries, like an adult trying to break through to a disinterested teenager. In this snapshot of their morning is hidden the definition of their coming relationship, which Ray Porter will come to understand almost two years later.

"You like your breakfast?" Ray decides to try a topic that is in both their immediate vision.

"Yeah."

"What do you usually have for breakfast?"

"A bagel."

"Where do you get bagels?"

"There's a shop around the corner from me."

Total dead end. He starts over.

"You're in great shape."

"Yoga," she says.

"I love your body," he says.

"I have my mother's rear end. Like two small basketballs covered over in flesh, that's what she said once, on a car trip." She emits a little chuckle. Ray gets an odd look on his face, and Mirabelle reads him and she says the only funny thing of the morning:

"Don't worry, she's older than you are."

He wants to reach over and slide his hand in between the opening in the robe that he has lent her. He wants to relive last night, to trace his hands over her breasts, to analyze and codify and confirm their exact beauty, but he doesn't. This will take place on another night with dinner and wine and walking and talking, where the seduction is not assumed, and the outcome undetermined. His sexual motor is already whirring and purring for their next date.

Ray's libido is exactly twenty-four hours ahead of his reason, and tomorrow at this time he will recollect that Mirabelle became quite helpless in the morning and wonder about it (his mind works slowly when it comes to women; he often does not know that he has been insulted, slighted, or manipulated until months or sometimes years later). But since he does not know what to expect from a woman – his four years of dating have not really educated him – he accepts Mirabelle's morning behavior passively. Ray's former experience has been with tough-minded, outgoing, vital, ambitious women, who, when displeased, attack. Mirabelle's dull inertia draws him into a peaceful place, a calm female cushion of acceptance.

He drives Mirabelle home, just in time for her to get ready and be late for work.

JEREMY'S ADULTHOOD

The stencil adheres to the amplifier by manila tape, and Jeremy has learned to evenly apply the paint in one skillful squirt of the airbrush. The Doggone Amplifier Company has a logo of a dog with cartoon speed lines trailing out behind it, with the brand name laid out in a semicircle underneath. It is not easy to fill in the delicate speed lines; some of the earlier paint jobs, before Jeremy joined the ranks, are uneven and sloppy. When he works he crouches in an uncomfortable position that only someone under thirty could bear for long before he would have to seek work elsewhere. His salary is so small that his paycheck could read "so and so measly dollars" and no one would contradict. But it's Jeremy's work clothes that tell the story of his line of business: his jeans look like a Jackson Pollock and his T-shirt looks like a Helen Frankenthaler – he is working at the bottom end of the arts.

His boss, Chet, ambles through the warehouse with a client in tow, and their faint muffled voices waft over the stacks of amps to Jeremy's straining ears. He catches a glimpse of them and notices that the client is a sharply dressed businessman, presumably the manager of a rock band trying to make a deal for a ton of amplification in exchange for promotion. The problem in the negotiation, of course, is that Chet only wants to sell amps, and the manager only wants them for free. There is no middle ground. Chet's business is waterlogged and about to sink and he simply can't afford to ship out fifteen thousand dollars worth of equipment for use months later. The manager slips away with a handshake and Chet stands there as the Mercedes disappears out of the lot through the chain-link fence.

For Christopher Columbus, it was the sailing of three ships that launched his life's great journey. For Jeremy, it is the sight of the sinking Chet watching the ass-end of a hundred-thousand-dollar car shrink to a vanishing point down an industrial street in Pacoima. He lays down his spray gun and gets in Chet's field of vision.

"You know what I was thinkin'?"

"What was that?" Chet barely replies.

"You know who hangs out with rock musicians when they're on the road?"

"Who?" says Chet.

"Other rock musicians."

"And?"

"If you had someone on the road with one of the bands using our stuff, someone who looks sharp, like that guy does ... " he thumbs in the direction of the dust of the Mercedes, " ... someone the musicians could relate to, I bet you could sell a lot more amps."

"Do you have someone in mind?"

"Me."

Chet looks at the specter of ineptitude that is standing in front of him. He does not see a sharply dressed businessman; he does not see a clever salesman. But he does see someone he thinks a rock musician could relate to.

"And how much would you like to be paid to do this?" says Chet.

"I could do it for ... "

Jeremy has never, ever been asked such a question. He has always been told what he would be paid. He can't even fill out an employment form that asks "desired salary" as it confounds him: he always wants to write down one million dollars. But Jeremy has been asked, so he has to answer:

" ... nothing."

"What do you mean, nothing?"

"I could do it for ... "

Jeremy has heard only one financial phrase in his life, and he opens and closes every door in his memory bank until he finds it:

" ... a finder's fee."

"And what would you find?" says Chet.

"Bands to use the amps. And if another band starts using the amps because of a band I got to use the amps, I'd like a finder's fee for them, too." And then hastily adds, "of five hundred dollars."

Chet can't see any reason not to take Jeremy up on his proposal. After all, it's a kind of commission basis, an Avon Calling of rock and roll. Since a set of amps can cost fifteen thousand dollars, it will be easy to shoot five hundred Jeremy's way. He doesn't see any problem in finding a new stenciler; in fact, his nephew is just out of high school and is looking for a job in the arts. Jeremy, overestimating his own value, is thinking the exact opposite: "I hope he doesn't realize he's going to have to find someone else to stencil."

Chet accepts the offer but does have to lay out some cash. Two hundred and twenty-two dollars for Jeremy to buy a new suit. Jeremy is enterprising enough to stretch the dough into an extra pair of pants so he won't look like a carbon copy of himself day after day. He then spends five dollars on a copy of *GQ* for his road bible on dressing and finds cool ways to manipulate his own six shirts into a weekly wardrobe. On the road, he learns to scan newsstands and surreptitiously tears pages out of magazines with ideas for style.

Jeremy's first gig is with the only professional band currently using Doggone amplifiers, Age – pronounced AH-jay. Age has scored some success with a one-shot hit record and Jeremy offers to accompany them for free in exchange for on-the-road amp repair. He will travel on their bus and bunk with a roadie. His real mission, of course, is to convince some other band, somewhere else, that he is a genius acoustician who has developed the ultimate amplifier and that Doggone amps are the only amps that any hip band can possibly consider.

Three days before Thanksgiving, he boards Age's auxiliary bus for a sixty-city road trip, starting in Barstow, California, heading toward New Jersey, and ninety days later, in a masterpiece of illogical routing, ending in Solvang, California.

THANKSGIVING

Ray and Mirabelle's subsequent date after the night of their consummation is as good as the first, but Ray will be out of town on Thanksgiving, so Mirabelle is forced to rely on her unreliable friends. She speaks to Loki and Del Rey several days before, who say they are going to a backyardfeast in West Hollywood, but they don't know the address yet and will call her when they get it so she can come. Several days before, she lays out her clothes for the occasion so she won't accidentally wear them too soon and have nothing to wear on the big day. Mirabelle's real ache comes from not being with her family, but it is either Thanksgiving or Christmas, and Christmas is the better and longer stretch during which to get away. Because of her unimportance to Neiman's she swings it so she can get a full five days off, assisted by a big lie that her brother's psychiatrist is going on vacation and the whole family is needed during the holidays to keep him straight. Mirabelle delivers this plaint to Mr. Agasa with a slight cry in her voice that says she is about to break down in tears. The genuine sympathy Mr. Agasa shows for Mirabelle's perfectly healthy brother embarrasses her, especially when he volunteers several book titles that link good mental health with exercise, forcing Mirabelle to dutifully write them down and file them in her purse.

On Thanksgiving morning, Mirabelle wakes with dread. She worries that there might be no call from Loki or Del Rey, which wouldn't be the first time they'd let her down and not thought twice about it. She can't dump them as friends because she absolutely needs even the slipshod companionship they give her. They are also her only source of party info, as she has been ostracized as a loner by the Neiman's girls. She waits till 10 a.m. to make calls to them both, leaving messages on their machines, asking for the address of the Thanksgiving dinner. At this point, Mirabelle foresees a disastrous day ahead of her unless one of these two flakes calls her with the address. First, she has no cash. Second, even if she did, she knows that everything is shut tight on Thanksgiving, except the classic diner that she would have to dig out of the Yellow Pages and perhaps drive to downtown L.A. to find. She opens her refrigerator and sees a Styrofoam box containing a skimpy half sandwich she had rescued uneaten from a lunch two days ago. Horrified, her brown irises narrow in on this leftover, which she sees as her potential Thanksgiving dinner.

She goes for a walk on the vacant, empty street in front of her house, hoping when she returns to see a flashing red light on her answering machine. There is absolutely nothing stirring in the short blocks around her house. She can hear activity, the slam of a car door, voices chatting, a dog barking, but these sounds are distant and disembodied. She passes the school yard near her apartment and hears the clanking of a chain, swinging in the breeze against a metal pole. She sees not a person.

By the time she angles her way back and up the stairs to her apartment, it is noon. From across the room, she can read that the light is not flashing, is not signaling an end to her worry. She goes back outside and repeats her thirty-minute walk.

This time, she calculates. She calculates the time it will take for Loki or Del Rey, once they retrieve the message, to actually call her. Once home, they will probably play the message within the first ten minutes of arrival. There might be other messages on their machines to return, there might be other things to do. This means that it will be a half hour from the playback to her phone call. Mirabelle knows that her walk is just a half hour long, and using a calculus discerned from Ray Porter, figures that there is going to be no new call on her machine when she gets back. So she takes a sideways turn and extends her walk by ten minutes.

When she gets home, she jiggles the door open and sees – out of the corner of her eye, not wanting to betray to herself her own anxiousness – the red light of her machine blinking at her in syncopation. She waits a minute before playback, occupying herself with a made-up kitchen chore. It is Jeremy, calling from the road, vaguely wishing her a happy Thanksgiving and simultaneously canceling out the thoughtfulness of his call by boasting that he's using the phone for free.

Mirabelle sits on her futon, knees to her chest, and sinks her head over. Her foot taps impatiently on the floor as the clock ticks over, first an hour before the party is to start, then an hour after the party is to start, then it rolls upward to 4 p.m., when darkness begins to creep around the edges of her windows. She gets out her drawing paraphernalia and during the next hour fills in a background of oily black and leaves the eerie, floating nude image of herself in white relief.

The phone rings. Any call will be good on this deadly day. As it rings, she glares at it, momentarily getting even with the caller for the delay, then snatches up the phone and listens.

"Hi. What are you doing?" It's Ray Porter.

"Nothing."

"Are you going somewhere for Thanksgiving?"

"Yes."

"Can you cancel it?" says Ray.

"I can try." She amazes herself with this answer. "Where are you?"

"Right now I'm in Seattle, but I can be there in three and a half hours."

Ray has felt at 4 p.m. what Jeremy once felt at midnight: the desire to be swimming in Mirabelle. Except that the distance is shorter from Seattle to Los Angeles than it is from Jeremy's to Mirabelle's when two people want exactly the same thing. Ray has a plane standing by, at a mere nine thousand dollars, and by the time she has hung up the phone he is out the door.

In the hours between the phone call and Ray's arrival, Mirabelle's body chemistry changes hourly, and sometimes a flash picture of deepest love coming her way bursts upon her consciousness. Mr. Ray Porter, twenty-eight thousand feet up, sees her two bright pink nipples resting on top of her cushiony flesh. But as diverse as these two images are, somewhere in ethereal space they align, and Ray and Mirabelle are in love on Thanksgiving Day.

Ray brings airplane food for two, which on the private service he uses isn't bad. Shrimp, lobster, fruit dessert all wrapped in Saran. They nestle on her bed with their feast spread around them, candles burning, and he tells her how beautiful she looks and how much he loves to touch her, and later, Mirabelle takes out the gloves he has sent her, stands before him wearing nothing but them, crawls onto the bed, and erotically caresses him with the satin Diors.

They make love slowly, and afterward his hand wraps around her waist and holds her. And even though the gesture is somehow compromised by a lack of final and ultimate tenderness, Mirabelle's mind floats in space, and the five fingers that pull her toward him are received into her heart like a psalm. It is a comforting touch, a connection however tenuous, that makes her feel attached to something, someone, and less alone.

Later, as the millionaire lies next to her in the too-small bed in the too-small room, with one arm around Mirabelle and a cat lying on his chest, they talk back and forth in small packets of conversation. Ray listens to her work woes, her car woes, and her friend woes, and Ray makes up a few woes to tell her in response. They talk back and forth, but their conversation is second in importance to the contact of his hand on her shoulder.

"Holidays can be tough on single people. I generally don't like them," says Ray.

"Bad for me, too," says Mirabelle.

"Christmas, Thanksgiving … "

" … all bad," agrees Mirabelle.

"Halloween I hate," says Ray.

"Oh, I like Halloween!"

"How can you like Halloween? You have to figure out what to dress up as, and if you don't you're a killjoy," says Ray.

"I like Halloween because I always know what to go as," says Mirabelle.

"What do you go as?"

"Well, Olive Oyl." Mirabelle implies a "stupid" after she speaks. Mirabelle says this without the slightest trace of irony, in fact, with glee that at least this one part of her life is solved.

Although he does not know it, Ray Porter fucks Mirabelle so he can be close to someone. He finds it difficult to hold her hand; he cannot stop in the street and spontaneously hug her, but his intercourse with her puts him in proximity to her. It presses his flesh against hers and his body mistakes her flesh for mind. Mirabelle, on the other hand, is laying down her life for him. Every time she jackknifes her legs open, every time she rolls on her side and pulls her knees up so he can enter her, she sacrifices a bit of herself, she gives him a little more of her that he cannot return. Ray, not understanding that what he is taking from her is torn from her, believes that the arrangement is fair. He treats her beautifully. He has begun to buy her small gifts. He is always thoughtful toward her, and never presses her if she isn't in the mood. He mistakes his actions for kindness. Mirabelle is not sophisticated enough to understand what is happening to her, and Ray Porter is not sophisticated enough to know what he is doing to her. She is falling in love, and she fully expects her love to be returned once Mr. Porter comes to his senses. But right now, he is using the hours with her as a portal to his own need for propinquity.

In the morning, at a coffee shop around the corner, Ray ruins everything by reiterating his independence, even clearly saying that their relationship is not exclusive, and Mirabelle, in a logical and rational mode and believing that she, too, is capable of random dating, agrees for both of them, then adds that if he does sleep with someone else, she should be told.

"Are you sure you want that?"

"Yes," says Mirabelle, "it's my body and I have a right to know."

Ray believes her, because he is naïve.

Ray stays in L.A. for three days, sees Mirabelle one more night, calls her twice, hurts her inadvertently one more time, levitates her spirit once, makes love to her again, buys her a watch and a blouse, compliments her hair, gets her a subscription to Vogue, but rarely, maybe twice, kisses her. Mirabelle pretends not to notice. When Monday finally comes, she goes to work, passing the perfume girls with confidence, inspired by the undeniable evidence that someone is interested in her.

VISITOR

"Can I take you to lunch?"

Mirabelle stands at her post, and before her is a man in his mid-fifties, a bit overweight, with short-cropped hair and dressed like someone who never thought one way or another about dressing in his life. Everything he wears is in the wrong fabrics for a Neiman's devotee, his belt is not leather, his shoes are catalogue-bought. A porkpie hat sits atop his head. He wears a synthetic palm tree shirt, cotton pants, and well-broken-in work boots.

"You're Mirabelle Buttersfield?"

"Yes."

"I'm Carter Dobbs, I'm looking for your father."

Mirabelle and Carter sit at the Time Clock Café. This time, her admirer, Tom, is missing from the tableau, but most of the regulars move in and out of their spots, as though an unseen movie director has yelled, "Places everybody."

A few minutes into the conversation and Mirabelle knows why this man does not belong, nor care to belong, in the matrix of Beverly Hills.

"I was in Vietnam with your father. I have been trying to locate him, with this address. . . . " He slides a paper toward her over the metal tabletop. Mirabelle sees that it is her home address, which has remained unchanged in twenty-eight years. "I've written him, but I never get a response," he says.

"Does he know you?" asks Mirabelle.

"He knows me well. There's never been a problem between us, but he won't answer me."

"Why not?"

"I think I know why, but it's personal, and I'm guessing he needs to talk to me."

"Well," says Mirabelle, "that's our address. I don't know why he won't get in touch with you, but I'm . . . "

"Are you going to see him?" Carter interrupts.

"Yes, I'm going to see him at Christmas and I can give him your card, whatever you want."

"Thanks. It's the ones that don't call back that need to talk the most."

"It was so long ago."

"Yes, sweetie. So long ago. Some do better than others, and I've just made it a mission of mine to reach my brothers, see if they're okay. Is your dad okay?"

"Not always."

Mirabelle tries to size up Carter. She has seen his type in Vermont, although Carter is clearly not from Vermont, with his Midwest nonaccent, flavored occasionally with a subtle drawl. Well-mannered, kind, moral. Like her father. Except that Carter Dobbs wants to talk.

Mirabelle's father, Dan Buttersfield, has never spoken to her about one emotional thing. She is kept in the dark about family secrets; she has never seen him angry. She has never been told anything about Vietnam. When asked, her father shakes his head and changes the subject. He is stoic like a good WASP from Vermont should be. The household was shaken when Mirabelle was seventeen when it was revealed that her father, whom she adored, had been involved in a sexual affair that had lasted for seven years. Mirabelle's emotional age was always five years behind her real age, so this information was received as if by a twelve-year-old. It struck her hard and made her bluff happiness for the next eleven years. This event fits exactly into Mirabelle's jigsaw puzzle of sadness still being assembled inside her. Having watched her mother's struggle, Mirabelle keeps a fear harbored inside her of the same thing happening to her, and when anything occurs in her life that is even similar, like a current boyfriend going back to an old girlfriend, she breaks.

Carter Dobbs walks her back to Neiman's. He gives her his card from Dobbs' Auto Parts in Bakersfield, California, and he squeezes her arm good-bye. As he turns away from her, she finally can name what disturbs her about him. He doesn't laugh.

GIRL FRIDAY

Mirabelle is tied up in Friday traffic, and this is only Thursday. She slogs along Beverly and misses every light. She fails to step on the gas at the exact nanosecond of the light change, and she gets honked at by not one but two drivers.

Locked in the darkness of her car, with the wipers set on periodic, she feels uneasy. The night scares her. Then the uneasiness gives way to a momentary and frightening levitation of her mind above her body. She can feel her spirit disconnect from her corporeal self, and her heart starts racing. She had felt its calling card months earlier, this unwelcome visitor in her body, who seemed to fly through her and then was gone. This time it is stronger than before, and it stays longer. It is as though her body is held down by weights and her mind is being methodically disassembled.

The stairs from her impossible-to-negotiate parking space to her front door are endless; she trudges from step to step. The door is heavy as she pushes it with the inserted key. Once inside, she sits on the futon for several hours without moving. The cat nudges her for dinner but she can't get up.

Mirabelle has been through this before, but the power of the depression keeps her from remembering that its cause is chemical. As has happened several years before, her medication is failing her.

The phone rings but she cannot answer. She hears Ray Porter leave a message. She drags herself to bed without eating. She closes her eyes, and the depression helps her sleep. Sleep, however, is not relief. The depression does not go away, politely waiting to come back in the morning when she is refreshed. It stays, and tonight it works on Mirabelle even as she sleeps, poisoning her dreams.

In the morning, she calls in sick, faking a flu, which is the closest expressible illness to what she is actually experiencing. By noon she has thought to call her doctor, who wants her to come in and who suggests that she is experiencing a pharmaceutical collapse. But the chemical malaise makes her disinterested even in getting well, and she feels the value of everything that has meaning for her slip away – her drawing, her family, Ray Porter. For the first time in her life, she thinks she might rather be dead.

The hours slip along, and she might have sat on her futon all day had the phone not rung around four. This time she answers.

"Are you all right?" It is Ray Porter.

"Yeah."

"I called you last night."

"I didn't get the message. My machine is acting funny," she lies.

"Do you want to have dinner tonight? It's my last night here for a while."

Mirabelle can't answer. Ray repeats himself:

"Are you all right?"

This time, she lets her tone speak for her. "I'm pretty okay."

"What's the matter?" says Ray.

"I'm supposed to go to the doctor."

"Why? Why do you have to go to the doctor? What's wrong?"

"No. I have to go to my ... I take Serzone, but it stopped working."

"What's Serzone?" says Ray.

"It's like Prozac."

"Do you want me to take you to the doctor? Do you want me to come over there and take you to the doctor?"

"I probably should see him... ."

"I'll come and take you."

Within an hour, Ray collects her, drops her off at Dr. Tracy's, and sits in his car, waiting for Mirabelle in a no-waiting zone in Beverly Hills. He can see the stream of people going in and out of this medical building and wonders how Mirabelle can afford such treatment, but it is a Neiman's employee benefit that provides her with a local doctor, and luckily, her doctor has moved from the valley, twenty miles from her apartment, to the Conrad Medical Building two blocks from her job. Ray sees a beautiful woman in her thirties exiting the building with a broad-brimmed hat pulled low over her face, hiding two freshly enormous lips. Ray Porter guesses there is a waiting period after injection while they deflate to an approximation of actual human form. He sees a vibrant Chiquita with her ass vacuum-packed into a yellow rayon wrap, her torso perched on two tree stumps. He sees what he thought didn't exist except as parody: a leather-skinned businessman with dyed black hair, his shirt open to his waist, and his chest laden with fourteen karat. He clinks as he darts across the street.

He sees a dozen or so women who have decided that overkill is best in the breast department. He wonders if they are kidding; he wonders if the men who adore them excuse their lapse in taste and love them anyway, or see them as splendid examples of woman as hyperbole. This is what he likes about Mirabelle; her beauty is uncultivated and he can trust that what is there at night will be there in the morning, too. He wonders what it is that makes him willing to sit in his car on a street, this millionaire, waiting for a twenty-eight-year-old girl. Is it his lust for her, or is something happening inside him that makes him care for her in an unexpected, unpredictable way?

He sees a family of tourists, with a sixteen-year-old daughter who is so purely beautiful that it makes him ashamed of the lewd image he fleetingly conjures.

Ray has very loose boundaries on what he considers fair game, although rarely has he allowed himself to dip below the arbitrary twenty-five-year-old watermark. What distinguishes him from the man with dyed hair who clinked across Bedford Drive a few moments ago is that whether he knows it or not, Ray is actually looking for someone. But he needs to be killed off several times by getting in too deep with the wrong person; he needs to break a heart and know that he has caused it, and to experience the sudden loss of interest that can occur within hours of a high peak of desire.

At this point in his transition from boy to man, he does not know the difference between a woman who is feasible and one who is not. This is still to come. Meanwhile, his eye roams around and focuses his unconscious on what can be a woman's smallest desirable quanta. The back of her neck seen in the shadow of her hair. The arch of her foot resting in an open sandal. An appealing contrast in the color of her blouse and skirt. These glimpses propel his desire, yet because he won't admit to himself how small the thing is that he wants, he inflates it to include her entire self, so he won't think of himself as a bad guy. Then a courtship begins, unconscious lies are told, and an enormously complex schema is structured, all to attain the mystery of an ankle that enters seductively into an oversize jogging shoe.

As Ray Porter sits in his car in this corridor of lust, where scores of women pass through his crosshairs, a desire for Mirabelle takes root and spreads. He reminds himself that she is not feeling well, but then again, she might be in the mood later, and in fact, a good fuck might be the best thing for her.

Mirabelle emerges from the Conrad Medical Building with a prescription-sized sheet of paper in her hand, comes over to the car, and explains through the lowered window that she will go across the street to the pharmacy to fill it. Ray nods and asks her if she wants him to go with her, she says no. When Mirabelle is halfway across the street, she hesitates and returns to the Mercedes. Ray lowers the window, and Mirabelle, shrinking her body like an embarrassed child, speaks:

"I don't have any money."

Ray turns off the car, goes in with her, and pays seventy-eight dollars for one hundred tabs of Celexa, the latest miracle of chemistry that should right Mirabelle's listing ship. Back in the car, he suggests that she stay at his place for the night. Mirabelle takes this as an expression of his caring, which it is. It is just that his caring is a potion, mixed with one part benevolent altruist and one part chimpanzee penis.

He drives Mirabelle up the winding roads into the Hollywood Hills as she sags lower and lower. The Celexa will take weeks to kick in and she knows it.

"Thanks for all this."

"That's okay," Ray says. "Are you feeling better?"

"No."

However, the thought that someone is taking care of her buoys her up exactly one notch from the bottom of her earlier depression. An intense headache begins to split her in half, and after Ray slots the car in the garage, he helps her to his bed.

If the headache had not appeared, Ray would have stroked his hand along her, down across a breast to her abdomen, and tried to seduce her. The headache keeps her from seeing the worst side of Ray's desire for her, and the worst side of men's desire in general. He is lucky he doesn't try, because she would have hated him for it.

Mirabelle sleeps motionlessly and silently, with her auburn hair splayed across her face and neck. Ray lies next to her, flipping the TV channels with the volume set to whisper, doing a crossword, looking at her – sometimes wondering if now would be the time to wake her up for her all-important sexual cure. But the night passes eventless, and eventually he nods off and sleeps fitfully until morning.

Breakfast is the same as usual, only this time Mirabelle's inactivity makes sense – she is ill. Ray is leaving town for ten days, and he carefully takes her home and waits while she assembles herself for her day at Habitat. Mirabelle begins to motivate herself toward cure, and she knows physical activity will be good for her.

"Are you going to be okay?"

"Yeah."

He hugs her tightly, with his palms squarely on her sturdy back, then backs out with a wave and a good-bye.

Mirabelle vacantly labors at Habitat, lifting and hauling Sheetrock and occasionally putting on a giddy face for her co-workers that hides nothing. She declines to go out for a beer even though one of the volunteers is flirting with her. In her depression, she has accidentally put on the perfect outfit for driving Mirabelle-watchers wild. The exact right khaki shorts with the exact right T-shirt with the exact right surface tension.

Ray calls her that night to check in on her. She is feeling ever so slightly better, even if only from the placebo effect of one pill and being freed, at least for the weekend, from the monotony of the glove department. Still, she sits essentially motionless through Monday morning, separated from suicidal thoughts by only a thin veneer. She struggles all weekend to keep it from cracking.

Weeks later, Mirabelle doesn't know if she is feeling better naturally or because the Celexa is working. It feels like a natural lift, and she wonders if she needs the pills at all. But she isn't stupid, and she recalls hearing that this is a common feeling, so she keeps taking the pills daily.

VERMONT

Christmas is approaching and she is making plans for travel to Vermont. She will leave on one of the worst flights imaginable, the red-eye to New York on Christmas Eve, connecting to Montpelier on a commuter flight at 8 a.m. on Christmas Day, and then take a bus 150 miles to home. Ray gives her the cost of the ticket east, as he figures Christmas is going to strain Mirabelle's budget and why not help her. He also slips her an extra $250 so she won't be a pauper in front of her friends. She already knows what she is going to give Ray for Christmas, the nude drawing she made of herself the night of her Thanksgiving despair, in which she is suspended in black space. And he knows what he is going to give her, a hand-picked blouse from Armani, which he bought for her knowing she would be absolutely crazy about it.

Mirabelle begins the nightmare of holiday travel with a phone call from Ray wishing her well, and a black sedan he sent to take her to the airport. Even flying at these inhuman hours, the sedan is the last sanctuary of calm before the holiday crowds engulf her. After several hours, the 747 to New York stinks from the perspiration of 400 passengers being rocked and rolled in the uneasy Christmas air. She transfers at JFK and finds herself aboard a prop plane that sits on the runway a full hour before takeoff. On descent to Montpelier, the plane bounces through a snowstorm and scares even the pilot. Mirabelle has to comfort the twenty-five-year-old, six-foot-four footballer who sits next to her, who quakes with every engine downshift and every crank of the flaps. Mirabelle herself is not nervous; it just doesn't occur to her that the plane can do anything but land, and she alternates between soothing the athlete next to her and reading a book.

By morning, after retrieving her luggage without help and hauling it to a shuttle that takes her to the bus station, she looks like a college student bound for home, or a ragamuffin. The bus, warm and cold at the same time, heads through the light snow. The riders are equally divided: some of them are like Mirabelle, exhausted travelers who had bumpy naps on interminable night flights, while the others are wide-awake conversationalists on the first leg of their exciting Christmas journey.

When the bus pulls into Dunton at 11:30 a.m., Mirabelle can see her older brother Ken standing inside the depot, wearing a bright red parka the size of an oil barrel. They say quick hellos as she runs from the bus to the car wearing her skimpy L.A. jacket; the freezing wind tells her that she has been in L.A. too long. Her brother shifts the lime green Volkswagen into gear and mutters a "hey kiddo," and then drives about five miles an hour on the icy roads. Ken is a policeman with an uncanny knack for tracking down criminals in his small town, mainly because he knows everyone and has a sixth sense for adolescents who might be headed in the wrong direction. She feels deep affection for her brother, although this has never once translated into honest conversation. She asks him how Mom and Dad are, and he answers truthfully, which is that they are unchanged.

Unchanged means this: Mom cannot imagine in this world that Mirabelle is having sex, and Dad ignores the subject entirely. Even though Mirabelle is twenty-eight years old, her status as a child in the house has never changed. Father to daughter, daughter to mother, the relationships are frozen in time, and it is this containment she felt nine years ago that squeezed Mirabelle out of the house and into California, where she could start digging in fresh dirt for her real personality. California doesn't matter, though, once she walks through her parents' door.

Moderation in all things, including success. Her dad supports his family well but has not succeeded past that. The house is small and paper thin; they have two old cars, but currently her father is on a rampage of relative success selling home products à la Amway. The extra income means a few things are being refurbished, and a plastic sheet covers the entire roof of the house waiting for dry weather so it can be repaired.

Catherine and Dan have been married for thirty-five years, and the stoic construct of their relationship has been broken only once, when Dan revealed his seven-year affair with a neighbor. Catherine collapsed, then fought, then resurrected the marriage with a quiet power and sophistication that she had not shown at any other time in her life or has ever shown again. The one who was broken, who did not recover, who did not understand, and who saw the image of her father crack and shatter, was Mirabelle.

Mirabelle did not know how to rebound from this betrayal, and Dan did not know that while he was cheating on his wife, he was cheating on his daughter, too. But she still needed to be loved by this man who had committed the unspeakable, and the push/pull she felt toward her father confused and stunted her.

Even before this episode, Mirabelle had feared her father, but she could never remember why. She does remember a shift in his manner, sometime after he returned from the war. She remembers a loving, even jovial man who became sullen and removed, and whom she learned to be cautious around. With quiet pervading the house, Mirabelle would retire to her room and read, thus beginning a lifelong relationship with books. But now all that is years ago. Now her father is much more congenial, as though something has softened, as though his resolve to be unreachable has eroded with time.

"So how're you doin' out there?" Her father sits in the easiest chair in the living room, and Mirabelle sits on the sofa, verging on relaxed.

"I'm fine, I'm still working at Neiman's."

"How's your art coming along?" Dan never sees her endeavors in art as frivolous, and as much as is possible for him, gets it.

"I'm drawing, Daddy. I've even sold some."

"Really? That's great, that's just great. What do they sell for?"

"The last one brought six hundred dollars, split with the gallery."

Mirabelle's mother brings a tray of Cokes into the room and just catches her daughter's modestly expressed boast. She looks askance at her, as if to say, "Can that possibly be true?" For some reason she feels the need to fake naïveté about this art thing that Mirabelle is doing. She pretends she doesn't get the preoccupation with it, that it is all beyond her understanding. The source of this self-deception is a mysterious and arbitrary decision to place certain arenas outside her realm of understanding, like the man of the house being simply unable to comprehend how to wash and dry dishes. The woman who had become a firewall of protection around her family when it was threatened now feels the need to play dumb.

The three talk on, then Dad suggests the family take

a walk around the neighborhood, which they do. He leads her by certain houses so he can call out to neighbors and show off his daughter, and Mirabelle becomes the daughter she was to him prior to the revelation of his affair. She hangs back behind her dad. Her pose becomes awkward, her voice weakens, she shyly says hello to familiar neighbors, and none of what she has seen and experienced in California is present in her demeanor. Catherine stands by, in wife mode, and Mirabelle looks at her and wonders where her own deep eroticism could possibly have come from.

After the family dinner, with her brother's wife Ella making it five, Mirabelle goes to her room and sits on the bed amid the relics of her childhood. Her mother's discarded sewing machine has been stowed in the room, and there are a few stray cardboard storage boxes stuffed into her closet, but otherwise everything is the same. A clock radio from the seventies, predigital, sits on her bedside table, in exactly the same spot it occupied when Jimmy Carter was president. The books that Mirabelle dove into when she wanted to vanish from the family are still in perfect order on her painted wicker bookshelf. The yellow glow from the incandescent overhead light washes over everything, and it, too, is familiar. Although she feels she is a stranger in the house, she is not a stranger in this room. This room is her own, and it is the only place where she knows exactly who she is, and whom she is fighting against, and she would like to remain in it forever.

She opens one of the storage boxes – cardboard drawers in cardboard chests – and sees piles of old tax forms, long past any purpose of being saved, a few ledgers, and some rolled-up Christmas wrapping. She kneels down, brushing dust off the floor, and slides open the lower drawer. A folded sweater and more financial flotsam. She sees an array of photos tucked inside another antique ledger. She picks it up and the photos spill onto the bottom of the box. She sifts through them and sees Christmas pictures of herself at five years old, riding on her father's neck. He is all smiles and clowning, her brother is nearby with a space weapon, and Mom is probably taking the picture. But the mystery for Mirabelle is, what happened? Why did her father stop loving her?

Mirabelle lies back on her bed holding the photos like a gin hand. Each one is a ticket to the past; each reveals a moment, not only in the faces but in the furniture and other objects in the background. She remembers that rocker, she remembers that magazine, she remembers that porcelain souvenir from Monticello. She stares into these photos, enters them. She knows that even though the same people and the same furniture are outside her door, the photo cannot be recreated, reposed, and snapped again, not without reaching through time. Everything is present but untouchable. This melancholy stays with her until sleep, and she loves being held by it, but she cannot figure out why these photos are so powerful beyond their obvious nostalgic tug.

The next day, she and her dad take a walk in the woods. In Vermont, no matter in which direction you go, you end up in the woods, so they go straight out their own backyard. The snow is crunchy and manageable. Mirabelle wears her mom's parka, which makes her look like someone has inflated her. Dad is all man in a furry vest and plaid shirt and lambskin jacket. After the "how's Mom" discussion in which little is said and nothing is answered, Mirabelle produces from her pocket the photographs, and hands them to him.

"I found these last night. Remember these?" She laughs as she presents them, to indicate their harmlessness.

After reaching clumsily for his glasses, which are inconveniently stashed under layers of insulation, Dan looks at the photos.

"Uh-huh." This is not the response Mirabelle is looking for. She had hoped for a smile or chuckle or flicker of some memory of pleasure.

"We were giggly," probes Mirabelle.

"Yeah, it looks like we are having a lot of fun."

He hands the photos back to her. She cringes at his disconnection from the events in the pictures.

Mirabelle suddenly knows why the photos have such a powerful effect on her. She wants to be there again. She wants to be in the photographs, before Easter, before the shift in his personality. She wants to be hoisted onto her dad's shoulders the way she was as a child; she wants to trust him and be trusted by him, enough that he would share his secrets with her.

"These were taken right when you came back from Vietnam, weren't they?"

Mirabelle has tried to open this door before. Today his response is the same as always.

"Not sure. Yeah, I guess."

The air bites them as Mirabelle and her father continue to walk. Then, coming to a clearing in the snowy forest, they grind to an uncomfortable halt. Mirabelle pushes a hand deeper in her pocket and fingers the card given to her by Carter Dobbs. The distance from the house gives her courage and she thinks now is the time. "There's a man trying to reach you," says Mirabelle. "He says he knows you."

She offers him the card. Taking it, he pauses in the chilling snow and looks at it, saying nothing.

"Do you know him?" Mirabelle asks.

He hands the card back to her. "I know him." And the conversation is over. But she had noticed something. When he was holding the card, he took his thumb and traced it over the name, and when he did so, he was powerfully distant from where he is now, in this snow with his daughter, in the woods in his backyard, in Vermont.

Her mother leaves the house to go babysit for her three-year-old grandchild. Mirabelle goes to her room after watching several hours of television with her now monosyllabic dad. The house is quiet, and she angles the shade on her bedside lamp and browses some of the books of her youth: *Little Women*, *Jo's Boys*, *Little Men*, *Jane Eyre*, *The Little Princess*, *Secret Garden*, *The Happy Hollisters*. Nancy Drew. Agatha Christie. Judy Blume: *Are You There God? It's Me, Margaret*. *Deenie*. *Starring Sally J. Freedman as Herself*. But something catches her ear. Something … the sound of a cat? Or an injured animal in the far distance. But her mind keeps recalculating the data, inching the source of the sound closer than the outdoors. This wail, these moans, are coming from inside the house. Wearing her bunny slippers – a gift last Christmas from an aunt who underestimated Mirabelle's age by fifteen years – she opens the door to her room and steps out into the hall. She does not need to walk far to know that the sounds, which she has now identified as sobbing, are coming from her father, who is behind the closed door of his bedroom. She stands frozen like a deer with bunny feet, then guides the slippers backward into her room, noiselessly. She shuts her door without making a sound, as she had done one night twenty-one years ago after hearing the same cries coming from the same room.

The moaning has stopped, and now the house is quiet. Mirabelle sits in her armchair and sees her parka, which has tumbled off the foot of her bed and onto the floor. She retrieves Carter Dobbs's business card. She approaches her parents' bedroom and lays the tiny business card up against the doorway. Then she quietly slides her way back to her own room.

Six months pass unnoticed as Ray and Mirabelle live in a temporary and poorly constructed heaven, with him flying in and out, visiting her, taking her to fine restaurants, then back to his place, sometimes sleeping with her, sometimes not. Sometimes he takes her home and says good night. She does not like sex when she has her period. When she feels depressed, sex can sometimes leave her sullen, so during these times there is an awkward domesticity while they wait it out. He takes note of her use of expressions that linger from her adolescence – lazy bones, sleepyhead, early bird – and is alternately amused and annoyed by them. A toothbrush is set aside for her. Since his house is closer to Neiman's, she often stays the night with him, bringing an overlarge purse stuffed with a change of clothes so she can go directly to work from his house. When he fantasizes about sex, he thinks of her and no one else.

Ray shows up one day on Mirabelle's message machine, saying he is in town and inviting her to an event in New York next month, and yes, she'll need a dress so let's go shopping. He takes her to Beverly Hills on one of her floating days off and they spend an erotic day shopping at Prada for something suitable. Ray glimpses her changing behind the flimsy screens, and when they get home, she tries on the dress, and then he fucks it right off her. Over the next several days, Mirabelle plans the trip, makes arrangements to get off work, and silently counts the days until takeoff.

JUNE

Ray Porter can't believe how much she is crying, and he wishes he could take back what he has told her. But the letter is in her hand, just barely, and she looks away from it as she drops it onto the bed. She tilts her head down and sobs like a child. He had written the letter because he wanted to say it succinctly; he didn't want to stammer or mollify it, he didn't want to change direction in the middle of a sentence and retract what he was about to tell her because of a vulnerable look in her eye. But she wanted to know; she had asked to know and she seemed to have meant it. So he handed her the letter in person as they sat in his bedroom, at the beginning of the evening, which quickly came to a close hours before it normally would have.

Dear Mirabelle,

I suppose the only way to say it is to say it: I slept with someone. It was not romantic or intimate, and I did not stay the night with this person.

I am not telling you this to hurt you, and I'm not

telling you because I want our relationship to change. I am telling you this only because you asked me to. I hope that you can find a place of understanding in you.
I am sorry,
Ray

With Mirabelle turned away from him, he takes the letter and quickly slides it into a drawer so she won't have to look at the tangible evidence of what he has done. The letter represents such an awful thing to her, and Ray does right by disappearing it.

He had debated with himself for two hours while flying to Los Angeles. Tell her, or not? But she had asked him to tell her. She must have meant it. Plus, it wasn't love; it was a fuck. Plus, she had asked him to tell her. He thought this was a new feminism thing that he is honor bound to oblige; that if he doesn't, he is a pig. That he will actually come off well by telling her; no one could judge him otherwise. But whatever his thought process was, whatever he told himself was the right thing to do, was false. Because his logic is not based in any understanding of her heart, and he continues to misread her.

Mirabelle doesn't ask any questions. She rises up and drags her sweater down the hall, stumbling like a drunk. Ray does not know how to handle this girl. If only she were practical, he would handle her in a practical way, but Mirabelle is in stage one – a child who has just had her heart rearranged by someone she trusted. She mumbles a cancellation of their upcoming weekend trip to New York. He follows her to her car and watches her drive away. The next day, he gets on a plane to Seattle.

⌾

Ray waits a day, then phones her just at the moment he knows she will be walking through the door.

"How are you?"

"Okay," she says in a small voice.

"You want to talk about it?"

"Okay. Can I call you back?"

"Yeah."

And they hang up. Mirabelle lays down her things, takes off her diaphanous Gap windbreaker, and drinks some water. She has been in a daze all day. She never wants to talk to him again, yet she is glad he called. She needs to talk to a friend, an ally, about Ray's transgression, but Ray is her only friend. She goes to her bedroom and dials area code 206.

"Ray?"

"Hang up and I'll call you back," he says.

"Yeah."

This is a fiscal ritual. Whenever she calls him long distance, they hang up and he phones her back so she won't have to pay for the call.

"Are you better?" he says.

"I'm a little better," she says, not knowing what she means.

"Should we see each other?" says Ray.

"I don't think so. I changed my ticket from New York. Is that okay? I want to go to Vermont to see my parents."

Mirabelle is not going to her parents for comfort. There will be no sympathy from her mother or father, because she can hardly explain the situation to them, especially since her father is guilty of the same act. But there will be solace in her room, in her things.

"Sure. Of course," says Ray.

The conversation stumbles on, and Ray tells her he is sorry he hurt her. And he is, but inside he doesn't know what he could have done differently. He is determined not to love Mirabelle; she is not his peer. He knows that he is using her, but he isn't able to stop. And as powerful as their desire for each other remains, their conflicting goals stalemate them, and their relationship has failed to move forward, even the incremental amount necessary for it to stay alive. They mumble some good-byes, Ray knowing it is not yet over, and with Mirabelle unable to think further than her own current pain.

PRADA

Lisa got wind of Mirabelle's Prada visit. For Lisa, Prada is the end-all be-all of courtship. Its exquisite clothes are not only expensive but identifiable. A Prada dress is a Prada dress and will always be a Prada dress. Especially a new Prada dress. A new Prada dress means that the trip to the shop is recent, that fresh money has just been spent, and if Lisa were wearing a new Prada dress, it would signify a big catch on her part. It would show that she has landed money and that her man has spent enough time with her to have escorted her to Beverly Hills and waited till she had tried on each and every, and then shoved a credit card thoughtlessly across the counter without even checking the price tag.

Lisa comes face to face with the rumor one morning when she sees Mirabelle arrive at work in a sparkling and flattering killer dress. To Lisa, Prada is as recognizable as her own mother, and seeing Mirabelle draped in the perfect Prada shift provokes in her a deep guttural growl. Lisa calls her friend at the store to get the full scoop, and yes, Ray Porter and an unknown miss did roll through. The only thing Lisa can think to do when she hears her worst fears confirmed is trim and coif her pubic hair. This is a ritualistic act of readiness, a war dance, that is akin to a matador's mystical preparations for battle. It is also done out of the belief that everything natural about her has to be tampered with for it to achieve its utmost beautiful state. Breasts, lip size, hair, skin color, lip color, fingertips and toenails, all need adjustment.

Lisa sits on the toilet as she shaves, one leg propped up on the bathroom cabinet. She can dip the razor in the toilet when she needs to wet it while she shapes and combs the furry patch to perfection. Lisa is determined to cull Ray Porter away from the Mirabelle mistake. All she has to know is where is he and what does he look like. She can easily glean this from the trusting Mirabelle, probably in one lunch, so she doesn't worry too much or make plans to connive. After the final dip of the razor in the toilet and a gentle splash of water to the now perfectly shaped lawn, Lisa stands up, stark naked, and looks at herself in the bathroom mirror. She is an hourglass with all the sand at the top. She is white and pink, and her implants pull and stretch and whiten the skin around them so her breasts glow. Her nipples are the color of bubble gum, and the silicone makes them resilient enough to chew like bubble gum, and now, between her legs, is the nicest little piece o' property west of Texas.

Mirabelle had told her parents that she was going to New York, so when she calls them and tells them she will be coming to Vermont instead, there is some explaining to do. But she bluffs her way through it, and since her parents never ask too many questions anyway, they are not aware that she can barely hold herself together.

On her arrival in Vermont, Mirabelle puts on an Academy Award face. She actually manages to appear cheery, though she occasionally retreats into her room to let the gloom from her losses with Ray Porter seep from her pores. She roams aimlessly through the house and sees on her father's desk the business card she had given him, significantly moved from the bedroom. She wonders if he has made the call that she hoped he would make.

Twenty-eight hours into her awful weekend, the phone rings and she picks it up. It is Ray Porter, calling from New York. There are awkward "how are you's," then, as he approaches his reason for calling, Ray softens his voice, giving the impression that he is leaning into her. He intones his question so apologetically it nearly brings them both to tears:

"Why don't you come to New York."

Mirabelle wants to be there, in spite of her ache, and there is no hesitation in her yes, as much as she tries to imply it. She has shown him that she is hurt, and now it is over. She wants to be in New York City, and not in Vermont.

Mirabelle tells her mother that she is leaving today.

"What on earth for?"

"I'm meeting Ray."

Mirabelle's mom and dad know that she is seeing someone named Ray Porter, but they pretend their daughter's relationship is somehow chaste. This of course requires incredible manipulations of reality and enormous blocks and blind spots. Mirabelle, to her mother and father, is simply not sleeping with anyone.

"Oh, that'll be nice for you," her mother says simply.

At this point, Mirabelle could have turned on her heels, and nothing more would have been said, ever. But 10,319 days have passed since her birth, and today for some reason, explicable only by the calculation of the stress of lying multiplied by twenty-eight years, Mirabelle adds one small truth:

"I'll be staying with him if you need to reach me."

Catherine continues scrubbing the same plate for the next few moments. "In a hotel?"

"Yes," says Mirabelle, and then, just for good measure, "but don't worry, Mom, I'm on the pill."

"Well," says Catherine. "Well," she says again.

Catherine rubs the plate, then in a modulation of voice so loaded with meaning that only Meryl Streep could duplicate it more than once, adds one more "well." With perfect theatrical timing, her dad walks through the kitchen door and she tells him the same thing all over again, just to feel the same rush of power one more time. But there is no clamor; instead, everyone sits on their churning feelings, and Dan quickly changes the subject, flips on the TV, and is then absorbed by it.

NEW YORK

She catches a plane that day and meets Ray in New York at dusk. Mirabelle doesn't have her Prada dress with her, but her quick instinct for clothes prevails and with an authoritative sweep through Emporio Armani assisted by a contrite Ray, who can't wait to atone by pushing wads of money across the countertop, she ends up swathed in a shimmering Armani silver dress that equals the Prada, and that night they head off to a dinner for fifteen hundred.

After the event, where she looks statuesque and elegant, where a few photographers' bulbs go off as they enter in spite of their noncelebrity status, where it is so challenging to Mirabelle to be sitting at a table for twelve among hundreds of tables, where she is so enthralled to be at this event that its dullness is not apparent to her, they end up at a small cocktail party for a dozen people at a smart Park Avenue apartment. The group gathers in a wood-paneled library where several Picassos look quizzically down on them. There are white-haired men older than Ray; there are sharp, young saber-toothed up-and-comers who have just cracked thirty. There are also tough businesswomen whose sexuality has somehow been packed away and left in a drawer somewhere and then, as an afterthought, stuck back on themselves and worn like a power tie.

They are a smart, agile-minded group, but they are not sure what to make of Mirabelle, who sits in the middle of them like a flower. She is the only one wearing anything lighter than dark blue. Unlike them, her white skin is a gift, rather than the result of being bleached under neon all day. Mirabelle speaks quietly and to individuals only. When someone finally asks her what she does, she says she is an artist. This leads to a discussion among the aficionados about current art prices that excludes Mirabelle from the rest of the conversation.

As the evening loosens, confounding the normal progress of a party, the conversations gel into one, and the topic, rather than jumping wildly from politics to schools for kids to the latest medical treatments, also gels into one. And the topic is lying. They all admit that without it, their daily work cannot be done. In fact, someone says, lying is so fundamental to his existence that it has ceased to be lying at all and has transmogrified into a variant of truth. However, several of them admit that they never lie, and everyone in the room knows it's because they have become so rich that lying has become unnecessary and pointless. Their wealth insulates them even from lawsuits.

All points of view are duly expressed, with nothing

new forthcoming, but with nods and asides and overlaps. This rapid exchange gives the appearance of an interesting conversation but one whose actual content is flat, dull, and drunken. That is, until Mirabelle speaks. Mirabelle, sober as an angel, fearlessly breaks into the chatter midstream:

"I think for a lie to be effective, it must have three essential qualities."

The booming voices of the men fade and the trebles of the women trail off. Ray Porter quietly worries inside.

"And what are those?" says a voice.

"First, it must be partially true. Second, it must make the hearer feel sorry for you, and third, it must be embarrassing to tell," says Mirabelle.

"Go on," the room implies.

"It must be partially true to be believable. If you arouse sympathy you're much more likely to get what you want, and if it's embarrassing to tell, you're less likely to be questioned."

As an example, Mirabelle breaks down her lie to Mr. Agasa. She explains that the partially true part is that she did sometimes need to go to the doctor. She then made him feel sorry for her because she was in pain, then she embarrassed herself by having to explain it was a gynecological problem.

The agile minds in the room click open the brain files and store this analysis away for future use. Ray Porter, meanwhile, is tilted momentarily one centimeter off axis and for the first time in almost a year wonders if it is not he, but Mirabelle, who is determining the exact nature and character of their relationship.

They don't make love that night, or for a while, but within a month everything resumes, and the letter and its dark information is mentioned only one more time, ever: Mirabelle tells Ray that if something similar happens again, it is better left unsaid. But the sandy foundation of their relationship has been eroded. It has been eroded by the unmentionable being mentioned; their silent agreement not to discuss Ray's devotion or dedication has been broken.

Mirabelle no longer knows what she believes about her relationship with Mr. Ray Porter. She no longer asks herself questions about it; she simply resides in it. Ray continues to see her and make love to her, with their erotic interest never waning, not even one pheromone. He pays off her credit card debt, which had whopped up to over twelve thousand dollars. Months later, he pays off her slowly accruing student loan, which has recently crossed the forty-thousand-dollar mark. He replaces her collapsing truck with a newer one. These gifts, though he doesn't know it, are given so that she will be all right after he leaves her.

He continues his quest elsewhere for a single appropriate love with occasional dates, road trips, and flirtations, but he continues to care about Mirabelle in a way he cannot explain. His love for her is not the crazy love he expects to feel, the swinging delirious rhapsody that he has promised himself. This love is of a different kind, and he searches his mind for its definition. Meanwhile, he maintains a belief that their relationship can go on undisturbed until the absolute right woman comes along, and then he will calmly explain the circumstance to Mirabelle and she will see clearly how well he has handled everything, and wish him well, and congratulate him on his reasonable thinking.

L.A.

"I'll have a hot dog," says Mirabelle. It must be noted that this is not an ordinary hot dog but a Beverly Hills hot dog with none of the unspeakable ingredients of a carnival hot dog. So Mirabelle is not violating the purity of the tender blood flowing under her dewy skin. Lisa, on the other hand, orders a salad that fulfills her personal view of the two main qualities of diet food: it looks ugly and tastes bad. She has not allowed that some foods, perfectly low in fat, can actually taste good. She saves ordering normal food, food that might not be so dietary, for those times when a man is watching, hoping to come off as a vixen who never gains an ounce. This is the importance of dating for Lisa; without it, she would wither away, barely able to lift a spoonload of sliced carrots.

Lisa and Mirabelle sit outside as usual, under the California sun on a perfect eighty-degree July day.

"How's your love life?" Lisa knows that her real inquiry is twenty questions away on her list, and she'd better start circling the topic early.

"It's fine."

"He doesn't live here, right?"

"He lives in Seattle."

"That must be hard."

"It's okay, we get to see each other once, sometimes twice a week, sometimes more or less." Then Mirabelle, oblivious to undercurrents and thinking that Lisa might have an interest outside Rodeo Drive, says, "Have you ever read *Idols of Perversity*?"

This question passes through Lisa like a cosmic ray: no effect. Mirabelle then does a neat and tricky little analysis of her favorite book while Lisa handles her disinterest by staring in Mirabelle's face and dreaming of makeup. As Mirabelle winds down, and as her break recedes into the land of lost lunch hours, Lisa pushes hard.

"When do you get to see him next ... ?"

Mirabelle never, ever would betray any personal information about Ray Porter, even his name, though in this case the fully briefed Lisa already knows it. But in her excitement she does tell Lisa that she will see him next week: "we're going to the Ruscha opening at the Reynaldo Gallery." Mirabelle assumes Lisa will be there already, as no one who attends anything ever at the the Reynaldo Gallery would miss the next event. In a clear instant, Lisa sees herself wrangle Ray away from Mirabelle and, with a simple toss of her lasso, utterly make him hers.

COLLAPSE

Ray Porter's quest for the right woman is not going well because he is living in the wrong eternal city. He is still in the city of his youth, where women in their twenties frolic like bunnies, and speak in high tones, and cajole him and panic him. He still believes that here he will find a china-skinned intellectual who will dazzle him with a wild laugh and a sense of life.

A bridge is being built in his subconscious. The bridge is to span from this eternal city to a very different eternal city. This new city is where his true heart will live, a heart that bears the marks of his experience, that knows how and whom to love. But the bridge is several powerful and painful experiences away from being finished, and right now he sits in his Seattle house with a woman he has no idea he isn't interested in.

Christie Richards is thirty-five and a fashion designer of some local note. She has a saucy body that given the right astrological moment and an exactly measured dose of Cabernet can arouse Ray's memory of adolescent backseat conquests. And as Christie sits across from him at his dinner for two, which has been prepared and delivered to the candlelit table by a nearly invisible chef, all the essential ingredients of lust converge on him. As he rotates her body in his mind so he can see it from all sides, Christie drones on about Seattle fashion.

"... but I want windows, because without windows you're a rack designer. I have an over-weight design that sells well, but no store is going to put an overweight design in their window, they want to bury them in the basement...." And she talks on and on, sometimes mentioning a recognizable fashion name as she continues to drink and pour, drink and pour, finally coming to the dregs of the Cabernet, with Ray, hiding his enthusiasm for getting her steaming drunk, casually opening another bottle and filling her glass.

But by the end of dinner, Christie starts talking with a slur, a big slur, and Ray begins to wonder if he has perhaps shoveled a few too many drinks her way. He takes her outside for some refrigerated Seattle air, which he thinks will do her good. It does her good, but not him, as now she is energized with oxygen and ready to forgo the foreplay, which at this point Ray Porter needs desperately if he is going to do what a man's gotta do.

She then drags him to his bedroom, which she has been in before, but only on a polite-host guided tour. The lights are already at dim and she kneels down before him and tugs at his belt buckle with the words, "I'm gonna suck your dick."

"Well, all right," thinks Ray. Christie fumbles unsuccessfully with the incredibly simple pants hook, then falls flat on her face with a kerplunk. On his wheat-colored carpet, she looks like a drunken *Christina's World* by Andrew Wyeth, except instead of the longing look toward the homestead, she is trying to focus her eyes on anything that will stay still. She brings her face to within one foot of the bed leg and gamely crosses and uncrosses her eyes, hoping to bring the swirling images into one.

Ray knows he is in the wrong place at the wrong time, even if it is his own house. He knows he shouldn't be doing this, he knows that the days of these parenthetical women appearing in his life sentence are coming to a close. He helps her up and walks her down the hallway to the living room, where he props her on the sofa, shoveling pillows under both her arms so she won't fall over. He looks into her eyes and says dumbly, "Can you drive?" He doesn't really say this to find out if she can drive, but to let her know it is time to go home. She, knowing her limits, shakes her head "no," although Ray isn't sure if she means no, or if she can no longer hold up her head.

Ray can drive her home but there is the car problem. Her car is parked outside, and if he drives her home there will be the morning headache of taxicabs and meeting times.

"You can stay here in the guest bedroom."

One of Christie's eyelids droops lazily. "I want to stay with you."

Ray is not amused with her. He firmly says no and

takes her to the spare bedroom. She, stunned, sees the door close on her. Then she turns, sees the bed and falls on it face first.

Ray Porter sinks into his thousand-dollar sheets as if he were sliding into heaven. He is alone and happy about it, but he does worry that Christie will feel her way along the hallway and find him. His usual speedy calculations slow to molasses, and big thick questions blob their way down his thought tunnel: How long does this go on? Why am I alone?

Ray is asleep, and dreaming of knocking. Knocking? He wakes at the moment of deepest third-stage slumber, so groggy that only one of his senses – his hearing – is functioning. He lies there, wondering if there is a burglar in the house. He pulls himself out of bed and walks down the hall, brave only because he quickly computes that the odds of there actually being a burglar are slim. He can hear the noise in the distance ... is it down the street? There is construction down the street; would they be working at 3 a.m.? He hears it again, but this time realizes it is someone knocking on his front door.

He pulls open the door and there is Christie, standing fully dressed, except she has no shoes.

"My shoes are in your backyard."

The only logical scenario is so illogical that he does not ask her what happened. She must have gone to the backyard, slipped off her shoes, decided to leave, left the house forgetting her car keys and been forced to knock on the door rather than sleep outside, or something like that. He gets the shoes, bundles up Christie, who is underdressed for the chilly night, puts her in his car, and drives her the eleven miles to her home.

The next day, he sends her flowers.

൭

Mirabelle puts on her pink argyle sweater and her pastel plaid short skirt to wear to the 5 p.m. Ruscha opening, and when she exits her car in the sheltered Beverly Hills parking lot, she looks like a rainbow refracted in the spray of a lawn sprinkler. At the far end of the lot, a car is being locked and a man steps away from it. In silhouette, he files a paper in his billfold. His suit tapers at the waist and his hair falls over his forehead. He starts to walk away, but Mirabelle is illuminated by the last remaining rays of yellow sunlight that stray into the garage, and she catches his eye.

Then he says, "Mirabelle?"

Mirabelle stops. "Yes?"

"It's me, Jeremy."

He approaches her at an angle, the light now raking across his face, and she can finally see him. Although he is the same person, this new Jeremy has nothing to do with the old Jeremy. It would take three Old Jeremys to trade in for one New Jeremy, as the New Jeremy is the sleeker, better model, with many desirable features.

"It's so nice to see you again," he says.

So nice to see you again? Mirabelle thinks, "What is he talking about?" This is not Jeremy lingo. Is she supposed to say "so nice to see you again" back? It isn't particularly nice to see him again, but it isn't unpleasant either, and she is curious about him. But before she decides what to do, Jeremy casually unbuttons his one-button suit, leans forward, and kisses a continental hello on one of her cheeks.

"Are you going to the opening?"

"Yes, I am," says Mirabelle.

"I didn't know if I'd make it back to town before it closes, so I wanted to see it tonight. Can I walk with you?"

Mirabelle nods, surveying Jeremy's sumptuous leather shoes and the precise fall of his pant legs draping over them. She wonders what happened.

What happened was this. Jeremy's three months on the road, which expanded into a year of multiple trips eastward, not only were a financial success, relatively, but were a success of another kind: Jeremy evolved from ape to man. After touring with Age for only a couple of weeks, Jeremy was invited to stay with them on their bus. After a gig, the bus would leave at around 1 a.m. and be driven three hundred miles or so to the next stop. Usually everyone on the bus would stay up a couple of hours, then retire to individual sleeping bunks with draw curtains that recalled a 1940s train, minus Ingrid Bergman. Inside the bunks were headphone jacks that plugged into a central sound system. One of Age's members was a Buddhist, new enough to the discipline that he went to sleep every night listening to audiotapes of books on Buddhism and meditation. Jeremy would plug in because he was bored. At first, he was sickened that he was listening to spoken-word tapes and wind chimes, but soon, after one particular meditation provoked a surreal vision in which he toured his bedroom at age four, the nightly routine became the high point of his evening and he began to listen, and listen intently. But more important, as the Buddhism tapes dwindled, new tapes from shopping mall bookstores were purchased from the same shelves that stocked the now exhausted supply of Buddhist recordings, and Jeremy was suddenly plugged into the entire current canon of self-help.

These books, listened to in the hypnotic rolling darkness of his Greyhound bunk, taught Jeremy about the Self, inner and outer, Jungian archetypes, the male journey and rites of passage, the female journey and rites of passage, the care of the soul, and Tantric sex. He got a heavy dose of relationship books, beginning with *Men Are from Mars . . .* and ending with a parody book called *Loving Someone Dumber Than You* (Jeremy identifying with the "you" and not the "dumber"). As the bus rolled on through Kansas, Nebraska, Oklahoma, and Nevada, under a million stars undimmed by city lights, Jeremy had his consciousness raised and therefore his life altered, by accident.

They walk across Santa Monica Boulevard and Jeremy explains the success of his business and how he is back in L.A. looking for a place to set up larger manufacturing quarters for Doggone Amplifiers. As he walks with her, he picks up her hand and says, "You look great; you really do look great."

This is what Lisa sees as she zeros in on them from fifty yards the other side of the Reynaldo Gallery: a man in a well-cut new suit holding Mirabelle's hand as they walk up Bedford Drive. And she assumes Jeremy is Mr. Ray Porter.

"Are you here alone?" Jeremy asks Mirabelle.

"I'm meeting a friend."

"Travel has left me friendless in L.A.," says Jeremy as he opens the door for her and escorts her in. Lisa slips in behind them and statistically becomes, at the already crowded party, the only woman there with a lavender perfumed cunt.

Five o'clock is early for a party, but not in L.A. where the average wake-up call is 7 a.m. Dinners are normally at 7:30 on the dot, which is perfect for a jet-lagged New Yorker who arrives and is eating at 10:30 his time. So this party is just starting to fill up, and many of the familiar faces are there. Artist/Hero is there, with a date this time, but he remembers Mirabelle and calls her over. Jeremy separates from her and goes to the bar for a newly discovered favorite, soda water, cranberry juice, and vodka. Lisa views this as Primetime and sidles next to him, overhears his order, and asks for the same thing. She waits till the drinks are delivered, then moves her aromatic twat within striking distance.

"Oh my God, I've never seen anyone else order one of these," says Lisa.

And she is off and running. She laughs at everything Jeremy says, which is difficult because Jeremy is not by nature a funny person. But Lisa knows that finding him funny is essential to her conquest of him, and she therefore finds herself chuckling even at his most innocuous utterances, including several observations about the current political scene. When she realizes these comments are serious, Lisa has to abort a grin midway and quickly twist her face into her version of profound concentration. Her assault continues, cajoling, poking him a couple of times, coyly dipping her tongue in her drink. Then she looks over at Mirabelle and says how insulting it must be for Jeremy to have her chatting up some other guy when the one she came in with is so attractive. "I have a secret," she says. "I know who you are. I'm Lisa by the way."

Since we all live in our own worlds, Jeremy assumes that word of his exploits and success with amplifiers has reached the coast. He loves that an attractive redhead has been informed of his savvy entrepreneurship, so when she says do you wanna meet later for a drink, he glances over at Mirabelle – which reinforces Lisa's erroneous belief – feeling unexpected regret that it was not she who had done the asking. But he gives Lisa a fact-finding once-over, and says yes.

Lisa laughs and flirts with him for another half hour then ups the stakes.

"Can you leave now?" she asks.

"Yeah, sure."

"What about Mirabelle?" says Lisa, feigning concern for another person.

"I do what I want," replies Jeremy, never thinking to mention that they are not a couple.

This comment releases a flood of estrogen into Lisa's bloodstream and has her dreaming of sex, babies, and a home in the valley.

Jeremy doesn't understand Lisa's aggressiveness but he doesn't need to. And neither does his recently elevated consciousness. There is no way the tranquil waters in which his brain floats so serenely can also calm two testicles of an unattached twenty-seven-year-old male.

"Let me say good-bye to her."

Lisa almost, but not quite, feels embarrassed. "Okay, but I'll wait outside."

At her apartment, which has been cleared of roommates by prearrangement, Jeremy gets the works from Lisa. He is shown the illustrated Kama Sutra of Lisa Cramer, cosmetics girl first class, with additional notes contributed by a dozen How to Fuck books, two radio psychologists, the gossip of two highly sexed girlfriends, articles in *Cosmo*, and an incredible instinct for arousing a man's superficial interest. He is slowly stripped and stripped for, he is levitated with oral hijinks, massaged and toyed with, rolled backward and masturbated, and finally finished off with a cosmic ejaculation while Lisa deep-breathes and chants. Afterward, Lisa's belief that she has just blasted the head off Ray Porter is reinforced when she asks if she is better than Mirabelle, and Jeremy, who has no idea that he is not Ray Porter, has no choice but to nod yes. After a customary but brief period of forced cuddling, Jeremy rolls out of her apartment with Lisa's last words being, "Call me."

◎

While Lisa thinks she is giving him the works, Ray Porter arrives at the art party, scoops up Mirabelle, and takes her to dinner, where their familiar and bottomless lust asserts itself. Driving to his house, he reaches under her jacket and between the buttons of her dress, where he feels the spongy resilience of her breasts. At his house, they are destined to make love but a conversation starts instead. A deadly, hurtful conversation that begins by Ray Porter casually reasserting his independence, talking to her like a friend who is in the know, as if she were his partner in finding someone else.

"I was thinking of selling the house here, getting an apartment in New York. I love it there. Every time I land I get a rush. There's a four bedroom I like that a friend is selling, big enough in case I ever meet someone."

He says it, and there is a message in it, but its cruelty is not intended.

Mirabelle tires. The speech, delivered as though it were an aside, drains her of momentum. Her arms dangle to her sides, and she drops into a chair. She knows this, she knows everything already, she has heard this. Why does he have to reiterate? To remind her that this is nothing?

She looks up at him and asks him a horrible question. "So are you just biding your time with me?"

The answer is awful, and Ray doesn't say it. He doesn't say anything at all, just sits next to her. Mirabelle's mind blackens. The blackness is not a thought, but if it could be pressed into a thought, if a chemical from a dropper could be dripped onto it causing its color and essence to become visible, it would take the shape of this sentence: *Why does no one want me?*

He pulls her into him, her forehead on his shoulder. He knows that he loves her, but he cannot figure out in what way.

So she sits there, her short fingernails digging into him, trying to hold on to something that will keep her together, that will keep her from flying apart in all directions. As she clutches him, she feels herself sinking into a cold dark sea and there seems no way out of it, ever. The proximity of the man she has identified as her salvation makes it worse. He takes her to the bed and she lies face down on the covers and he rests his hand on the small of her back, occasionally stroking her. He tells her that she is beautiful, but Mirabelle cannot align this thought with his rejection of her.

The next morning, Lisa picks up the ringing phone.

"Hi. It's Jeremy."

"Who?" says Lisa.

"Jeremy."

"Do I know you?" says Lisa.

Jeremy jokes, "When do you really know someone." Getting no laugh, he continues, "Jeremy from last night."

Lisa goes through the list of men she spoke to last night. None is named Jeremy, though sometimes men will find her and call her because they think they've made eye contact with her when they really haven't.

"Refresh me," Lisa says.

Jeremy is dumbfounded at the possibility that all his exploits, all his catapulting, could be so quickly forgotten by morning. He continues, "Me, Jeremy. I was at your place last night. We did it."

Something all wrong dawns on Lisa, "Oh, Ray!"

When Jeremy hears "Oh, Ray," he presumes it is slang or pig Latin or some contemporary expression of elation that has gotten by him. So he says it back: "O, ray!"

"God, you were great last night," offers Lisa.

"O ray," says Jeremy.

"What?" says Lisa.

Jeremy, involved in a conversation he can't follow, finally asks, "Do you know who I am?"

"Sure, you're Ray Porter."

"Who?" says Jeremy.

"Ray Porter, from last night."

"Who's Ray Porter?"

"You are . . . ," then she adds, "aren't you?"

In the morning after the agony of the night, Ray drives Mirabelle to her car, in time for her to get to work by ten. He watches her walking stiffly away from him, overdressed for the morning, bearing her anguish so solitarily. He wonders if it will be the last time he will ever see her.

She puts on her driving glasses and starts up her new-for-her Explorer. She waves a small-fingered good-bye to Ray, and he notices her diligent concentration on driving as she pulls away.

She enters Neiman's, passes the disgraced Lisa, walks up four flights, and slides into her niche behind the counter. She stands there for the rest of the day, again stunned by an inexplicable world, her movements limited to those that her body has memorized.

Ray and Mirabelle's relationship does not collapse that day; it subtly dwindles over the next six months. There are fits and starts, but they can all be graphed on a downward slope. He takes her to dinners, drives her home, hugs her goodnight. Sex is over. Sometimes, she tells him he is wonderful and he presses her closer to him. She accepts a date with a sports equipment rep but she cannot offer him even the little bit required to keep him interested. Ray finally grasps that he is giving her nothing and that he has to think for the both of them and separate from her. He pulls back and she reflexively, protectively, does the same. For a while, Mirabelle believes there will be a moment when he will cave in and let himself love her, but eventually she lets the idea go. She hits bottom. She dwells in the muck for several months, not depressed exactly, but involved in a mourning that at first she thinks is for Ray but soon realizes is for the loss of her old self.

She is lying on her bed, day having passed into night without her ever getting up to turn on a lamp. She lights a candle in her darkened bedroom and is held in its tender illumination. Outside, sounds from surrounding apartments transition from dinnertime to TV time to quiet time. Her depression has consumed all of its fuel. She is exhausted from doing nothing to heal herself. As the darkness and solitude surround her, she drifts into communication with her smartest self. She admits that her college days are over, that her excursion into Los Angeles was transitional, and that Ray Porter is a lost cause.

It is morning, and Ray Porter's phone rings.

"Hi, it's me," says Mirabelle.

"Hang up, I'll call you back."

"No, that's okay," she says. "Guess what. I'm going to move." There is a lilt in her voice that Ray is not used to hearing.

"From your apartment?" says Ray.

"To San Francisco."

There is a short discussion about why she chose San Francisco, which is unrevealing, and there is no discussion about whether it's a wise move or not, as Mirabelle's determination is clear and strong. She makes one small request of Ray that he fulfills: she utilizes Ray's long chain of pull to land an interview with a gallery in San Francisco – not to be an artist with the gallery, but a receptionist. On Del Rey's ancient computer, she secures an apartment over the Internet and also makes contact with two potential roommates. Within three weeks she leaves Neiman's, whispers a good-bye to Los Angeles without looking back, and settles into a small flat in the Presidio district near the Golden Gate Bridge. Ray is surprised by her sudden movement, as she had seemed so frozen.

Mirabelle still faces difficulties, but Ray finances her move and eases a situation that even with his aid reduces her bank account to a long string of zeros, put the decimal anywhere. Her new job as receptionist recreates the kind of tedium she endured at the glove counter, but at least she gets to be ambulatory. And the mean age of the customers is lower by twenty years.

Another plus: the San Francisco arts scene is livelier

than the intermittent one in L.A. Every third night there's something going on somewhere, which she can either attend or pass on and curl up in her own bed. The gallery action puts her in the center of a glut of testosterone. Mirabelle is a ripe, relative virgin, and her romantic life starts badly. At an art opening, she meets an artist named Carlo who courts her for a month, fucks her several times, and leaves her cruelly: she calls him on the phone, he says he is on the other line and that he will call her back, but he never does. Ever. She summarizes and explains this event to herself not by saying that she is yet again unwanted, but that she has learned something about her own decisions. She has learned that her body is precious and it mustn't be offered carelessly ever again, as it holds a direct connection to her heart. She sheathes herself in a protective envelope of caution and learns never to give away more than is being given to her. The mini-disaster of this brief romance accomplishes something else, too: Mirabelle is able to shift her anger from Ray to Carlo, and Ray is then able to become a friend.

While she adjusts to San Francisco Mirabelle's spirits rise and fall, but she is determined to stay positive. Ray keeps in touch by phone and sends small checks her way when he reads the need in her voice. Mirabelle has long given up her instinct to refuse the aid, as she has no choice but to accept it, which she does with sincere humility and graciousness. She also pursues her art with a steady diligence, and her drawings are accepted in several group shows. The small drawing, not even eight inches square, of her lying nude floating in space is shown as being from the collection of Mr. Ray Porter.

In Mirabelle's new job, she meets artists and collectors. She is always careful not to promote herself through gallery contacts – her sense of correctness prevents it – but she now enjoys being a relevant person at the openings. She often calls Ray, who immediately calls her back according to plan. One afternoon she announces, "I'm going to an opening tonight and my goal is not to be a wallflower." Toward the end of each week, she has collected a few stories to report to him: her nights on the scene, who flirted with her, who slighted her. She also monitors the sporadic comings and goings of the vilified Carlo, who popped into one opening with a pregnant girlfriend on his arm, sending the fragile Mirabelle into an angry snit. She tried to get even with him through psychological warfare but couldn't, because he didn't care.

Mirabelle's stay in San Francisco stretches into several seasons. The frequency of her calls to Ray Porter diminish. She has a few flirtations, conversations really, that never amount to much. But one night, she takes the walk up the stairs of her new flat and notices on the doormat a small, oblong, clumsily wrapped box with an overly large Hallmark card taped to it. Once inside the apartment, she sets the box down on the kitchen table. She feeds the cats, then untapes the ends of the wrapping and inside finds a plain white box, and inside that, a rather cute Swatch watch. She opens the note and reads, "I would like to have dinner with you, Jeremy." And quickly scribbled below is the usually tacit implication, "my treat!"

Jeremy has been working around the West Coast for the last six months, during which time he's made an out-of-proportion six-year psychic leap by funneling the entire contents of the Bodhi Tree bookstore into his brain. He has been commuting to San Francisco ever since he hit the road and now, ready to settle down in L.A. and become a minor lord of amplifiers, he finds himself having to go to Oakland every week on business. Occasionally, Mirabelle's image floats into his consciousness and hangs there. The image he sees is not from his early pathetic dates with her but from his encounter with her in the parking lot on the night of the art party. Because not until then had he matured enough to recognize her as something beautiful and something worth holding as an object of real desire. He's found her by calling her old number, then looking up the new number in a reverse-directory on the Internet to find her address.

Mirabelle calls him at the number scrawled on Jeremy's note, her memories of the awkward night in her apartment also having been diluted by their short walk to the Reynaldo Gallery, now almost a year ago. A date is set several weeks in the future. When the day arrives, he shows up in a taxi, and from her window, Mirabelle sees him tip the driver several generous bucks. They walk to a local restaurant where, upon approaching the hostess, Jeremy announces, "Table for two, Mr. Kraft." Mirabelle has forgotten his name is Kraft but is aware that this is only the second man in her life who has taken her to a restaurant where a table has been reserved for them.

Mirabelle does most of the talking, and Jeremy listens intently without saying much. Later, Mirabelle will remember the dinner as the time she first found him to be very interesting.

On the walk home, as they warm up to each other and the night, Mirabelle recites the litany of reasons for her move, leaving out the most important one, and gets down to a final summation:

"I'm fixing myself."

"I'm fixing myself, too," says Jeremy.

And they know they will forever have something to talk about.

While Jeremy dates Mirabelle and makes tiny inroads into her, Ray continues to occasionally see her. In an act of self-preservation, she no longer makes love to him, and because he finally cares about her fully, he doesn't try.

Mirabelle takes months to accept Jeremy, and Jeremy patiently waits. And as he stands by, his feelings for

Mirabelle grow. One night, she cries in his arms when a recollection of Ray flirts with her memory, and he holds her and doesn't say a word. Where his insight comes from as he courts her, even he doesn't know. It might have been that he was ready to grow up, and the knowledge was already in him, like a dormant gene. Whatever it is, she is the perfect recipient of his attention, and he is the perfect recipient of her tenderness. Unlike Ray Porter, his love is fearless and without reservation. As Jeremy offers her more of his heart, she offers equal parts of herself in return. One night, sooner than she would have liked, which made it irresistible, they make love for the second time in two years. But this time, Jeremy holds her for a long while, and they connect in a deep and profound way. At this point, Jeremy surpasses Mr. Ray Porter as a lover of Mirabelle, because as clumsy as he is, what he offers her is tender and true. That night, coming up for air from the unexpected love he is falling in, he gives some opinions on tweeter wholesaling that Mirabelle secretly calls "the second oration." After he nods off, she pokes her forefinger into his closed fist and falls asleep.

Their union is the kind of perfect mismatch that makes for long relationships. She is smarter than he is, but Jeremy is in love with his own bright ideas, and the enthusiasm he shows for them infects Mirabelle and pushes her forward into the world of drawing for money. She begins to enjoy tolerating his enthusiastic outbursts; this is her gift to him. Sometimes they lie in bed and Mirabelle relates the entire plot of a Victorian novel, and Jeremy is so captivated and engrossed that he believes the events in the story are happening right now, to him.

Mirabelle informs Ray that though she is cautious, perhaps she has met somebody. "I tell him about my medication and he doesn't care," she says. This is the moment Ray has always known is coming, when she succumbs to the unrestricted, unbounded, and free-flowing passion of someone who is her peer. In spite of its predictability, he still feels this moment as a loss, and a curious one: how is it possible to miss a woman whom you kept at a distance, so that when she was gone you would not miss her?

Ray also wonders why it is she and not he who has met someone accidentally in a Laundromat, someone who stumbles into your life and forever alters it. But just three months later, it happens to Ray – it isn't a Laundromat since he hasn't seen one in thirty years, but rather a dinner party – a forty-five-year-old woman, divorced with two children, touches his heart and then breaks it flat. It is then Ray's turn to experience Mirabelle's despair, to see its walls and colors. Only then does he realize what he has done to Mirabelle, how wanting a square inch of her and not all of her has damaged them both, and how he cannot justify his actions except that, well, it was life.

Jeremy and Mirabelle, who are not living together but are close to it, have shorter and shorter separations as he commutes south and north. Mirabelle and Ray continue to talk weekly or more, and they begin to be able to discuss the details of each other's romantic lives. On the phone, Mirabelle mentions that she wants to fly home to Vermont for a three-day weekend. She does not ask him for money – she never does – but Ray is always forthcoming when he senses her need. This time, however, he does not volunteer the dough and they chat on and hang up. He needs to sort something out.

As he stands on his balcony overlooking Los Angeles in the dusky orange sunset, Ray ponders his continuing concern for Mirabelle. If she is no longer seeing him, if she is now with someone new, wouldn't it be the new man's responsibility to pay for the odd necessity? Ray always had paid; he saw it as his gift to her, but now it is over. Yet he is still compelled to help her. Why?

He turns his powers of analysis away from the logic of symbols, and toward his churning subconscious. He strips his questions down to their barest form, and he finds the single unifying theme of his contradictory feelings. He suddenly knows why he feels the way he does about her, why she still touches him, and why, at irregular and unpredictable intervals, he wonders where she is and how she is doing: he has become her parent, and she his child. He sees, finally, that as much as he believed he was imposing his will on her, she was also imposing her need on him, and their two dispositions interlocked. And the consequence was a mutual education. He experienced a relationship in which he was the sole responsible party, and he notes its failures; she found someone to guide her through to the next level of her life. Mirabelle, standing on uneasy legs, now feeling the warmth of her first mature reciprocal love, has broken away from him. But he knows that like a parent, he will be there for her, ever.

Some nights, alone, he thinks of her, and some nights, alone, she thinks of him. Some nights these thoughts, separated by miles and time zones, occur at the same objective moment, and Ray and Mirabelle are connected without ever knowing it. One night, he will think of her as he looks into the eyes of someone new, searching for the two qualities that Mirabelle defined for him: loyalty and acceptance. Mirabelle, far away and in Jeremy's embrace, knows that what had been lost is now regained.

Months later, after the hard edges of their breakup had smoothed into forgetfulness, Mirabelle speaks with Ray Porter on the phone. She tells him about her new life, and he hears the fresh delight in her voice. She tells him, "I feel like I really belong here. For the first time, I feel like I really belong." She underplays Jeremy's place in her heart as she thinks it might hurt Ray. She mentions that she continues to draw and sell, with a positive review in *Art News* to her credit. They reminisce about their affair and she tells him how he helped her and he tells her how she helped him, then he apologizes for the way he handled everything. "Oh, no ... don't," she corrects him: "it's pain that changes our lives." And there is a pause, and neither speaks. Then Mirabelle says, "I took the gloves to Vermont and stored them in my memory box – my mother asked me what they were but I kept it to myself – and here in my bedroom, in my private drawer, I keep a photo of you."

Acknowledgments

If writing is so solitary, why are there so many people to thank? First, Leigh Haber, who delicately edited the book without bruising my ego; Esther Newberg and Sam Cohn, who first uttered encouraging words; my friends April, Sarah, Victoria, Nora, Eric and Eric, Ellen, Mary, and Susan, who were all convinced that it was their idea to read and provide helpful comments on this book during its early stages. How can I thank them except to offer a twenty-five percent discount on bulk purchases when accompanied by a valid driver's license?